Steph reached the pharmacy's white-painted steel door. The *open* pharmacy door.

She froze in disbelief. She remembered locking up the night before. That's when she'd turned and nearly bumped into Hal. She blushed at the memory. But she had closed and locked the door.

Hadn't she?

A chill ran through her. A vise of tension wound itself around her head. Her heart beat louder and her breath came in short spurts.

"Easy," she murmured. No reason to freak out. Not yet.

Careful not to let her fingers touch anything, Steph kneed the door ajar. She slipped inside and headed for the cabinet where she kept the narcotics locked up. But before she got there, she caught sight of the empty shelf against the back wall.

The pseudoephedrine was gone. Her worst nightmare had come true. Her thief was making meth.

Books by Ginny Aiken

Love Inspired Suspense

Mistaken for the Mob
Mixed up with the Mob
Married to the Mob
*Danger in a Small Town
*Suspicion

*Carolina Justice

GINNY AIKEN

Ginny Aiken, a former newspaper reporter, lives in Pennsylvania with her engineer husband and their three younger sons—the oldest married and flew the coop. Born in Havana, Cuba, raised in Valencia and Caracas, Venezuela, she discovered books early, and wrote her first novel at age fifteen while she trained with the Ballets de Caracas, later known as the Venezuelan National Ballet. She burned that tome when she turned a "mature" sixteen. Stints as reporter, paralegal, choreographer, language teacher and retail salesperson followed. Her life as wife, mother of four boys and herder of their numerous and assorted friends, brought her back to books and writing in search of her sanity. She's now the author of more than twenty published works and a frequent speaker at Christian women's and writers' workshops, but has yet to catch up with that elusive sanity.

Ginny Aiken
SUSPICION

Steeple
Hill®

Published by Steeple Hill Books™

STEEPLE HILL BOOKS

Steeple
Hill®

ISBN-13: 978-0-373-44319-2
ISBN-10:   0-373-44319-6

SUSPICION

www.SteepleHill.com

Printed in U.S.A.

For I have kept the ways of the Lord; I have not done evil by turning away from my God.
—*Psalms* 18:21

To Lynette Eason, a real-deal friend,
for helping me stay sane in a year of insanity.

ONE

Loganton, North Carolina

"It looks even more ominous out there than it did fifteen minutes ago."

Pharmacist Stephanie Scott shuddered as she stared out the front window of her general store/pharmacy again. September could bring nasty weather into her mountainous corner of the Carolinas, and that purply black sky in the early evening meant nothing good.

She turned to Jimmy Miller, her stock clerk. "You can go ahead and leave. It's ready to storm."

The sixteen-year-old's freckled face brightened with a grin. "Cool, huh?"

"Only if I'm indoors—which is where you better get going unless you want to become a lightning rod."

With a wave, Jimmy ran off, and Steph resumed her nightly routine. She tallied up the prescriptions she'd filled, cross-checked her computer list against her handwritten log and relaxed when everything matched up. She then locked her controlled-substances cabinet, brought down the metal grate over the counter, twisted the combination knob, left the pharmacy part of the store and then secured that door as well.

With her purse over her right shoulder and the night-deposit sack under her elbow, she latched the front of the store, set the alarm and slipped out the back. The satisfying *snick* of the dead bolt gave her a sense of security each and every night. She'd done everything she could to protect the community from drug thieves. That was a major source of concern and topic of discussion among pharmacists of late.

As she took the key from the regular door lock, an unexpected *scritch* sounded behind her.

Steph froze. Before she could turn, she was shoved off the back steps. She flew through the air, the key clutched tight in her fist. She landed on the filthy asphalt alley floor by the communal Dumpster, banging her right leg against the cold metal.

Pain stole her breath, but she knew what she had to do.

"Help!" Steph yelled, so loud her face throbbed from the effort.

A dark figure launched itself onto her back. The sharp blow from a knee to her spine took her breath away. Her attacker's weight on her middle flattened her against the ground; the upright position gave the mugger advantage over her.

"Give me the key," her attacker said in a guttural whisper.

Steph squirmed, tossed, bucked and kicked, all the time holding the key in her fist. She shoved her hand between her abdomen and the asphalt, out of the mugger's reach. The rough surface ground away at the skin on her knuckles. With each kick at her assailant, the knees of her pants ripped more. At no time did she stop screaming.

At no time did her assailant stop beating. Her shoulders and the back of her head felt each blow twice, once when her attacker struck and then again when she hit the alley floor.

Time, however, did stop. Steph registered pain, the heavy weight on her back, the dampness of rain, the stench of trash…and something vaguely spicy and sweet laced in with the rot. Her fear-filled mind couldn't identify it, but she knew it was there, somehow familiar, just beyond her grasp, important but elusive.

And still the pounding continued.

In what felt like hours, but could only have been a handful of seconds, Steph sustained blows on the head, her back, her arm and both legs. The alley surface scraped her face each time it touched down.

"What's going on here?"

At the sound of local postmaster Andrew Cooper's deep bass voice, the person on Steph's back paused in his assault.

"Who are you?" Steph bucked one more time. "Why are you doing this?"

"Steph?" Mr. Cooper said. "Is that you?"

Her attacker stood.

Seconds later, footsteps pelted away as the first cold raindrops splashed on Steph's sore back.

"Who's there?" the postmaster called again, this time closer to Steph.

She rolled to her side. "Please call 911, Mr. Cooper. Someone tried to mug me."

The portly gentleman trotted up and knelt at her side, cell phone in hand. "You hurt, missy?"

"I don't think it's serious, but we do need the PD."

Dialing, Mr. Cooper tsk-tsked. "My first thought was about you." He put the device to his ear and waited for a response. "I'll have us someone here, pronto— Yes," he said into the phone. "There's been a mugging behind Scott's Pharmacy…"

With help on the horizon, Steph's eyes welled with tears.

Who would have done this? Loganton wasn't a particularly crime-prone town. Besides, it was no secret she didn't make a great deal of money.

On the other hand, her pharmacy was rich with drugs, which she kept under lock and key. True, her professional bias immediately brought that to mind, but for what other reason would she have been attacked? Even someone who didn't know her could verify with a minimum of effort how little cash she kept in the store. They could also watch her make the two deposits every day, one at lunchtime and the other after hours.

While Loganton was relatively clean by comparison to larger cities, in the past couple of years the town had experienced a scattering of drug overdoses, and last spring Ethan Rodgers and his fiancée, Tess Graver, had nearly died at the hands of a meth dealer.

Under the worsening rain, Steph unfurled her right hand. In her damp palm, within four half-moon indentations etched by her nails, lay the key to the door. "Thank you, Jesus," she whispered.

She'd kept the drugs where they belonged.

At six o'clock, Hal Benson slid into his usual booth at Granny Annie's Diner, the only eatery in Loganton. Even Pepper, his rescued greyhound, turned up her elegant nose at the cooking.

As he settled back against the puffy red vinyl seat, Karla, Granny Annie's youngest niece, skidded to a stop by his booth, glass of water, order pad and red ink pen in hand.

Hal grabbed for the water in self-defense.

"Hey, Sheriff Hal!" Karla's cheeks glowed pink, her brown eyes sparkled and her riot of black curls fought the restraints of the hairnet her part-time job forced her to wear. "You want the same as always?"

He took a drink as he thought for a minute. His frequent meat loaf, mashed potatoes and whatever vegetable Granny Annie offered that day didn't really appeal to him tonight. "What's the special?"

"Granny's got two. Spaghetti, salad and garlic bread's one, and the other's chicken potpie, biscuits or corn bread and spiced apples on the side."

"Hmm…the chicken sure sounds good. Why don't you bring me some of that?"

"Iced tea?"

"Is there anything else a man would want with his meal?"

Karla laughed. "Not this sheriff, I guess."

Hal took another sip of water then glanced out the window. The sky was ripe with the incoming thunderstorm. He hoped it would pass quickly; otherwise he was in for a drenching by the time he left the diner. Then he chuckled. If that was the worst thing he had to face that evening, he'd get off lightly.

Karla zipped off to the kitchen.

A flock of customers sailed in. The flurry of greetings inspired by their arrival filled the diner with the comfort of familiarity. Out of the corner of his eye, Hal saw Karla tear back out from behind the counter with her tray perched on a slender shoulder.

"Beep-beep!" She smiled at the newcomers in the aisle. "Beep-beep!"

Before the lively young waitress reached his booth, Hal's cell phone rang. "Sheriff Benson here."

"Hey, sir?" Patsy Anderson, his newest deputy, had a little-girl voice and the tenacity of a bulldog. "I'm not sure about this, but since you're already out there for supper, I thought you might want to know."

Hal held out a hand to slow Karla. "I want to know. What's up?"

"Well, sir, it seems when the pharmacist, Miss Scott, went to close up tonight, she got mugged—"

"I'll be right there. And thanks, Patsy." He turned to Karla. "Can you have Granny hold my supper for me? I've got to go on a call."

Karla rolled her eyes. "As if this was new."

He sighed. Having Granny Annie hold his meal until after he'd taken care of whatever latest problem had erupted was not new. What was new this time was the victim.

Steph Scott had been mugged.

Hal hurried out, hopped into the cruiser, drove down Main Street, cut across River Run Road, then turned into the alley behind the pharmacy. He parked by the white Loganton PD car already there.

Veteran officer Wayne Donnelly and his rookie partner Maggie Lowe stood on one side of the back steps to the pharmacy, while Mr. Cooper, the postmaster, stood on the other. Steph sat on the top step, visibly shaken. All three were drenched by the now steady rain and blowing wind.

While Maggie smiled a greeting, Wayne frowned. Steph looked scared.

Hal tapped the brim of his hat, working to hold his concern at bay. "I was about to eat supper at Granny Annie's when my deputy called. She figured since I was close by, I might be interested in what happened. I know you guys have jurisdiction, so I'm not here officially, unless you want my help, that is. Just came to offer, since Granny Annie's is so close."

Steph glanced up at him, her gray eyes huge. "All help is welcome," she said, her voice low.

Hal shoved his hands in his pockets. That was that. It would now take an act of congress to budge him. "What happened?"

Maggie turned. "It sounds pretty typical. Steph was closing up shop when the mugger attacked. She fought him and was able to keep him from getting the key to the store."

Out of the corner of his eye, Hal saw Steph shiver. "Hang on."

He ran to his cruiser. There was no reason for her to be cold as well as hurt when he had an unused jacket in the car. The abrasions on her face were bad enough.

"Here." He held out the navy waterproof coat seconds later. "You need it more than my trunk does."

For a moment, he thought she'd argue. It wouldn't surprise him if she did. He'd watched Steph put everyone else's needs before hers for years now, even back when they'd both been in school. She'd always been the one to help rather than the one who received the help. This time, however, she was in need.

Hal was about to insist when she surprised him by reaching out and taking the jacket. Their fingers grazed in the exchange, and the electric shock of awareness that hit him took his breath away. From the startled look on Steph's face, it seemed she'd felt it, too.

For a moment, Hal wanted nothing more than to reach out, wrap his arms around her and promise her everything would be fine. But he couldn't do that, so he did the next best thing. He held out the coat for her.

As she slipped her arms into the sleeves, he said, "We're going to make sure we get the guy who did this to you."

Her silvery-gray gaze met his. "Thanks."

"Of course we will," Maggie added, giving Hal a curious look.

He blushed.

With a shrug, she turned back to Steph. "Don't suppose you have surveillance out here?"

Steph shook her head.

"Wouldn't be a bad idea. We might have caught the guy on film."

"I'll think about it."

"You do that," Maggie said. "Let's get back to what happened here. You're going to have to tell us everything you remember, every last detail. We never know what might be important in an investigation."

"I understand," Steph said. "I made sure everything inside was locked up as it should be before I walked out the back door. I took care of the dead bolt first, then the regular door lock. I was about to put my key chain into my purse, when…"

Her words faded off into the rush of the wind, and shudders shook her. This time, Hal couldn't hold back. He reached an arm around her shoulders, offering the only thing he had to give right then: his comfort and support.

She met his gaze again, and he had the strongest urge to smooth the silky-blond bangs away from her eyes. But again, he couldn't do that. For right now, his arm around her shoulders had to be enough.

Then Steph took a deep breath. "I'm pretty sure he was after the key to the store. He didn't touch my purse. That wasn't a regular thief. I think he was after drugs."

Hal nodded. "Loganton's drug problem seems to be growing. But I'm determined to clean up the mess in my county."

Maggie chuckled. "Is that another one of those famous campaign promises, *Sheriff* Benson?"

Heat rushed into his cheeks. "Okay. So I am running for reelection. And, sure, I've made drugs a major plank in my campaign. But I hate the damage substance abuse brings down. And it's not just the abuser it hurts, but it's also the whole community that suffers. It's a real issue." He shook his head. "It's not just a campaign promise, Maggie. It's my personal commitment to shut down the drug trade that's wormed its way into my jurisdiction."

As he spoke, the sweet smile he liked so much brightened Steph's pale face. "I'm so glad to hear that, Sheriff Benson. I've been doing what I can to educate the kids for the past few years."

His heart kicked up its beat. "I can always use a partner in my camp."

She gave a quick nod. "You've got one. Let's get this creep."

Easy, Hal, easy. She's only promised to work with you to catch a mugger. But he was hungry for whatever he could get. He also knew if the Lord so willed, much could come from a tiny seed.

"Yes, let's catch this creep before he strikes again, Steph Scott."

The minute Hal uttered the words, a niggling thought crawled into the back of his mind and a hollow feeling into his gut. Just how did he plan to make good on his offer? He couldn't imagine there'd be clues in the alley or footprints on the wet asphalt surface. There wouldn't be fingerprints to lift since the mugger hadn't touched anything but Steph's back.

What if he couldn't catch him?

He had not only an election to lose, but he also stood to lose the chance to know Steph better. He'd first noticed Steph in school, in third or fourth grade. He'd been too shy all through their teen years to approach her, even though his interest in her had only grown. Now, after all that time he really wanted to help her. And maybe get to know her. What better way to do that than to catch the guy who'd mugged her?

But, of course, there was always the possibility he'd fail.

The creep might be long gone. Could he catch someone who'd left not a trace behind? Could he keep the light of trust in Steph Scott's eyes from burning out?

On Wednesday, the day after the mugging, Steph spent the morning preparing prescription refills for residents at The Pines, a nearby retirement community, between the orders that came in over the phone or as regular drop-offs.

At two fifteen, Chad Adams, the new driver and delivery-man for Pharmaceutical Suppliers and Mr. Cooper's much younger brother-in-law, came up to the counter and rapped his knuckles on the window.

"How's it going, Steph?" he asked, scrubbing his ultrashort buzzed red hair.

"Same as always, Chad. Do you have a lot for me today?"

He chuckled. "Oh, yeah. Let me get to it, but first…" He plunked down his daily ration of red licorice ropes.

Steph rang it up, gathered his dollar and change and headed to the back room to check off the purchase order as Chad brought in the product. Once they were done, she sent Jimmy to sort and restock shelves as needed.

"Well, hello there, boss!" Darcy Thomas, Steph's best friend since forever, burst into the store, her usual energy radiating from her every pore. She blew a bubble, and the pink stuff popped, never catching her lips or cheeks. She had a gift of sorts. "Whatcha got for me to do today?"

Darcy's mother had died a little more than a year ago. The numerous courses of cancer treatments had wiped out any savings the two women had accumulated, leaving Darcy with a pile of bills to pay, including funeral expenses. Steph had offered her friend the opportunity to earn a few extra dollars by helping her on Wednesdays, when the store tended to be its busiest and she and Jimmy couldn't keep up by themselves.

At four o'clock, Jimmy ran past her pharmacy counter in a hurry to stow his broom in the back storage room. "They're here, Miss Steph!"

She glanced up and down the aisles of her store then turned to Jimmy. "Looking good! You did a nice job. Every shelf is full, and the aisles are clear and clean. We're ready for them."

Within seconds, the bell she'd hung on the front door clanged, announcing her customers' arrival. A river of senior citizens flowed in, each one with a shopping plan in mind.

"Hey there, sunshine!" Mr. Mason Cutler called out. "It's my lucky day. If I have to take blood pressure medicine, at least I get to see the prettiest girl in the Carolinas whenever I pick it up."

Steph handed him his bag of pills. "You're too much of a flatterer, Mr. Cutler. But I love you anyway."

Miss Patience Doolittle, former school principal and professional spinster, as she identified herself, sidled up to the window. "Don't you pay any attention to the old coot, Steph. He'll yap your ear off if you let him."

It never changed. The two should have married decades ago, but for one reason or another they hadn't figured out they couldn't live without bouncing ideas and arguments off each other.

Yet.

She still held out hope for them.

Steph smiled. "Here you go, Miss Doolittle. I have your arthritis meds ready for you."

"Hey, Steph!" Darcy called. "Any more of those padded insoles? Seems everyone's dumping their sandals for real shoes, and the things are flying outta here."

Steph gave her directions to the stash of extra foot-care products. Then she went back to her queue of senior citizens.

The next hour rushed by as it always did. Before long, the antacids shelf was bare, the lotion, cologne and dusting powder area lay ravaged, and the neat pyramid of nutritional supplement shakes she'd had Jimmy construct ten feet away from her counter had been reduced to its two bottom rows.

Dawn Stallman, activities manager at The Pines, plunked down a bottle of shampoo, two boxes of tissues and a non-prescription antihistamine product on the counter. "I think they're about ready to move on to our next invasion."

Steph rang up the handful of items. "I don't mind them. I think they're sweet and wonderful."

"Oh, they are. But they're the quirkiest bunch you could imagine, too. And I love them."

With a smile, Steph handed Dawn her bagged purchases. "I'll be out to give my talk on skin care on Saturday afternoon."

"Thanks. You've really made a difference. Most of them are taking better care of themselves since you started your preventive-care program. And you will touch on diabetics' skin problems, right? They listen to you."

Steph nodded. "It's not a big deal. They've all done so much for their families and the town…the least I can do is help them raise their comfort level now that their bodies have begun to give out."

After a hearty round of goodbyes, Dawn marched her troops out to the retirement community's bus, and Darcy darted off to Miss Tabitha Cranston's boarding house, where she worked as the housekeeper. Scott's Pharmacy grew silent again—too silent. Steph loved what she did. And every struggle it had taken to get to where she was these days had been well worth the effort. She felt God had called her to serve Him by caring for His children's medical needs.

"Hey, Miss Steph," Jimmy said. "Would you just take a look at this? It's ruined. Who would do such a thing?"

Steph leaned across her counter behind the pharmacy window and reached for the blood pressure cuff box the teen held out. One corner had been cut away with almost surgical neatness and precision. Her stomach sank.

This was the sixth damaged package they'd found after four weeks' worth of Pines residents' Wednesday shopping trips. Problem was, Steph couldn't imagine any of her seniors in the role of vandal.

She sighed. "Let me have it. I'll have to check it out."

When she'd opened for business, Steph had been determined to offer the most reasonable prices possible and still make enough profit to keep the pharmacy open.

In five years of business, she'd avoided all vandalism. Sure, every once in a while she noticed the typical shoplifting kind of attrition, but no actual malicious damage. Until now. These many ruined items in four weeks weren't typical.

Then again, there was nothing typical about the night before. She'd never felt any danger while at her store, but she'd been mugged. A thought crossed her mind. She stared at the box with its cutout on the side. Could there be a connection between the mugging and the vandalism? Should she report this to the detectives? It didn't seem particularly important, but they'd told her to notify them if she thought of any detail, no matter how seemingly insignificant.

This certainly fell into that category.

If it turned out to be nothing, she'd feel totally stupid. But if it was connected to the mugging, and she didn't call the cops, then they might be missing a potentially crucial clue.

Steph sighed. She had to call the PD.

Again.

A few minutes later, the pop of Mimi Larson's ever-present bubble gum came over the phone. "We'll have someone out there right away," the Loganton PD's dispatcher said. "It doesn't sound like much, Steph, but I guess I can have the officers check it out for you."

In spite of Mimi's dismissive assessment, Steph couldn't deny the uneasiness in her gut from the moment Jimmy had handed her the torn box. She knew the store's true rate of attrition. Six items in four weeks wasn't it. And such neat, surgical destruction?

No way was that normal. Even if it didn't make any sense.

This was her little world, everything she'd worked so hard for. She'd overcome all the issues that came from her attention deficit disorder so as to finish her schooling. Then she'd had to work hard to raise the seed money. The licensing tests had posed a monumental challenge, and all the other hurdles she'd had to jump in order to open her store had nearly gotten the best of her. But she'd stuck it out. She wasn't about to let some dishonest crook tear down her efforts now.

When the CB radio in Sheriff Hal Benson's department cruiser crackled, he listened, even if it was only to eavesdrop on one of the police departments in his county. Like now.

"Delta-202," Mimi from the Loganton PD said.

"Go ahead," Wayne Donnelly answered.

"Steph Scott at the pharmacy's reporting what might be vandalism…but it's kinda weird."

Hal bolted up in his seat. Steph? Vandalized?

He turned the cruiser around on the side road and listened more intently.

"10-4. It's kinda quiet today. I'll go check it out."

"10-4, Delta-202. And thanks."

Hal was tempted to turn on his siren, but who in his right mind used a siren for a vandalism call? Especially when the local police could and would handle it just fine. Still…

It was Steph who'd called. And she'd been mugged last night.

While it was just too pathetic to still be carrying a torch for the little blond girl three desks down from his in fourth, fifth, even tenth grade, Hal knew how he felt. He'd never found a woman who made his heart beat faster than the way Steph Scott always had.

If someone had hurt her, he had to help. Two calls in two days to the pharmacy were unheard of. And two too many, period.

He reached Scott's in less than ten minutes. He didn't want to think how many speed limits he'd obliterated to do so. But when he strolled in, he realized how foolish his rush had been. Wayne had everything under control, talking to Steph while Maggie inspected the store.

Well, everything except for the two tiny lines between Steph's eyebrows. Which prompted Hal to speak. "Anything I can do to help?"

Steph and Wayne spun.

"Oh, hello, Sheriff Benson," she said.

Wayne frowned. "Any problem, Benson?"

Hal shook his head. "I was near—" the county wasn't *that* big "—and I heard the call on the radio. Just thought I'd stop by and see if you needed a hand. After all, Steph was mugged yesterday, and the radio call just caught my attention."

Wayne jutted out his chin. "Don't know that there's much to see here. Just six messed-up boxes in four weeks. Maybe one of the seniors at The Pines was clumsy checking out the merchandise more'n Miss Scott would like when they come shopping. Maybe they thought trimming the damage they did might make it look like less."

When no one agreed, he shrugged and went on. "Doesn't look like much to me, even if Miss Scott here thinks it might have something to do with the mugger. I say folks are careless. Sometimes they're just plain crazy, too. Either this is some- one's idea of a prank, and it's downright mean, if you ask me, or stuff fell and got shoved around in the store."

"That's never been my experience," Hal said. But at Wayne's deepening frown, Hal hurried to add, "Still, it's just like I said. I was close…but of course, I'm sure you have everything under control."

You're the one who doesn't have anything under control, his conscience taunted with right-on-the-money accuracy.

On his way out, a thought occurred to him. "Did you get those security cameras yet?"

Steph gave him a look of disbelief. "When would I have had the time?"

"You might want to hurry things up. It might help you keep things under control."

Control. One little word, but, oh, how much it encom- passed. The PD had things under control. He was suggesting ways for Steph to keep things under control in her store. He sighed. The only thing not under control was him.

What was he doing here? No one needed him. He had a job to do.

He glanced at Steph again. There was just something about her that inspired him to leap tall buildings, stop speeding bullets—all the clichés. With a quick salute, Hal stood to the side, letting the efficient cops do their job. But no matter how hard he tried, he couldn't make himself leave.

Irritated, he called himself the biggest fool in town.

Yet another cliché: he was a fool in love. Still, how could it be love when he hadn't shared much more than passing greetings with Steph?

What kind of crazy am I?

TWO

"Before you go…" Maggie Lowe said as Steph stood to leave once the three law enforcement officers were done with their questions. "I suspect you'll want to know what we just found inside the blood pressure cuff box."

Steph shoved her bangs off her forehead then rubbed her palms, one against the other, and laced her fingers together. "A blood pressure cuff, I hope."

The officer gave her a wry smile. "It was there. But you already knew that. It's what we found behind the cuff that's so interesting."

Sheriff Benson crossed his arms. "You found something in the box?"

Officer Donnelly faced the other man. "Crazy as it sounds, there was a twenty-dollar bill shoved behind the cuff."

"Huh?" *Great!* First she came across as the weak little victim who got knocked down, and now she sounded dumb. "I mean, money? There was cash inside the box?"

Maggie nodded. "It was an old bill, so when we check it for prints I'm sure we'll find plenty of them—too many, actually. And then, when I called Dawn Stallman from The Pines, thinking one of the seniors might have…oh, I don't know, felt guilty and stuck it in there to make up for the broken box, she says no one would fess up. She did ask all the seniors who came in today."

"That is strange," Steph said.

The sheriff uncrossed his arms. "I don't think the twenty's a case of conscience. The folks out at The Pines wouldn't do that. They'd take the box they broke right up to the counter and face Steph—er…Miss Scott."

"It wasn't broken," Steph said. "Someone cut into that box with a very sharp blade. Deliberately."

Maggie nodded.

Sheriff Benson turned to Steph. "Who else came into the store today?"

She groaned. "I can't begin to remember. Let's see… Miss Tabitha picked up her prescription, and I remember Mr. Holcomb stopping in for his little girl's insulin…" Steph frowned, concentrated and eventually came up with a list of about ten customers. Then she shook her head. "I'll have to check my records to see who else picked up prescriptions. We can look at the checks and credit-card slips in the deposit bag, too. That'll give us a better idea who was in the store."

"Sounds good to me," the sheriff said. He turned to the two police officers. "How about I follow her home? I can look at that bag. She—" he faced Steph "—*you* can make the deposit in the morning, right?"

As strange as it seemed, Steph felt relieved to know the sheriff, even though practically a stranger, would come home with her. She just didn't relish walking into her little carriage house behind the Farmer's Supply Store alone. The local farmer's co-op had turned the town's century-old livery stable, a lovely, historic building, into the wire-and-feed-and-more store, but by this time of night it was also dark and empty. For the first time she realized how isolated her home, the original livery owner's home, was all the way out on the edge of town.

"I'll stop by the bank on my way to work tomorrow morning," she said, heading for her car. "And if it's okay with all of you, I'd like to close up shop now."

Damp from the rain and shivering from an excess of nerves, Steph couldn't wait to be rid of the whites she wore to work. Fortunately for her, Loganton was small. It only took seven minutes to get home. In no time, she pulled her car into the garage, snagged her purse and deposit bag and locked up her gas-efficient compact car. She waited for the sheriff just inside the garage door, then, once he met her, used her garage-door remote to lock up behind them.

"I'm sorry to keep you so long," she said as she went up the steps to the inside door. "This whole thing is just unbelievable…very unusual. But you can go on home now. I'll get the list of customers to you in the morning."

He gave her his brief but sincere grin, which lit up his brown eyes and deepened the crinkles at their corners. "Don't worry about it. We're partners in the battle against drugs, remember? Partners help partners."

Steph stepped into her tiny kitchen, much too conscious of the tall sheriff's presence at her back. What would he think of her home? It was, after all, an ultrafeminine nest by design.

She shivered and her teeth chattered. Were the tremors the result of the dousing she'd gotten outside? Or did the adrenaline from her natural fight-or-flight response, to first the mugging and now the theft, get the better of her? Or was her sharp awareness of her companion's striking presence to blame? She took a deep breath then gestured toward her glass-topped iron bistro table and the two chairs with their heart-shaped backs—all she could fit in the small space. "Have a seat. Can I get you a glass of water? Iced tea?"

"Iced tea sounds great." He pointed to the deposit bag. "And I'll get started with that list of customers while you change into dry clothes, so I can get out of your hair as soon as possible."

Steph handed over the blue simulated-leather pouch, poured the sheriff a tall glass of tea and then ran to change. She couldn't stand another second in her clammy clothes. Five minutes later, she was back, dressed in dry khakis and a cream-colored sweater.

"Sorry about that," she said. "How many names did you come up with?"

"Here." The sheriff turned his notebook so she could read it. "It's not a particularly enlightening list."

Steph scanned the names. "I see what you mean. I can't picture any of these people vandalizing anything, much less beating me up."

Her thready voice must have betrayed her exhaustion because he gave her an appraising stare. "Are you sure you don't want to go stay with your parents? Will you be okay here by yourself?"

"I'm fine—tired, and sore from last night's mugging, but that's what ibuprofen is for, and I hear Scott's Pharmacy has a good supply." She smiled. "I've got an in there, so I don't need to worry Mom and Dad. I'm okay."

An awkward silence descended on the room. Steph studied the list of her customers' names, the most convenient place to keep her gaze. She'd never had a man in her home before. This felt very strange, especially since she didn't really know Hal Benson very well, and even though he'd come in his official capacity.

True, she remembered him from back in school; they'd graduated the same year. He'd been the class brain, while she'd been the one who stared out the window when the slightest thing distracted her, the one who made teachers despair. Then, after high school, she'd gone to UNC at Chapel Hill, where a kind and wise learning disabilities counselor worked with her, while Hal had headed for Princeton. How and why he became a sheriff after all that, she didn't know.

"Umm...I guess I'd better get going." He pushed away from the table, making his chair's metal feet screech against the ceramic tile underfoot. He winced. "Sorry about your floor. I'm outta here. You do need to rest."

She waved away his concern. "Oh, don't worry about that. Tile is pretty tough stuff. But you're right. I do need to rest."

He stood in place, looking around the room, his cheeks reddening, clearly disoriented.

Steph chuckled. "Follow me. You don't have to go out my back door. This is a funky little place, but it suits me just right." She headed to the front. "Don't try to tell my parents that, though. They're convinced I should still be living at home."

His laugh warmed her almost as much as her dry clothes had. "Family around these parts has long strings, doesn't it? My parents stopped guilt-tripping me only when they decided to buy one of the cottages out at The Pines. I'm too young to live over there."

At the front door, Steph turned and met the sheriff's gaze. "Thanks again."

He dipped his head. "It's all in a day's work."

It struck Steph how shy Hal Benson really was. That explained a lot, like how they'd managed to go through school together and she still knew practically nothing about the man.

The earlier awkwardness returned. A hunted look crossed the sheriff's craggy features. Steph's natural response was to reach out, to say something to put him at ease, but she realized this wasn't the right time.

Next time she saw the appealing sheriff, she'd make sure to reach out and make an extra effort at friendship. He seemed to be one of the truly good guys.

"Well," he said when the tension grew tighter than the wire the Farmer's Supply sold. "I'll be in touch. As soon as we know something…"

"I look forward to hearing from you. I'm sure you'll catch the mugger. And figure out this box-slashing thing, too."

And she was. Hal Benson struck her as a man who wouldn't give up until he'd met his goal. With his natural intelligence, she doubted much ever got the best of him.

"Thank you for your trust, Miss Steph—"

"Now, really." She cut in with a smile. "You've known me since I wore that sloppy braid that never stayed tight back in school. I think you can drop the miss. I'm just Steph."

His eyes twinkled. "Good night, just Steph. I'll see you soon."

"Good night, *Hal*. I'm sure you will."

Steph locked the door behind the sheriff. After the echo of his footsteps melted into the rumble of the rain against her roof, the overwhelming silence shrouded her.

Funny how she'd never noticed the profound quiet of the area around her home. She loved the small home with its angled rooflines and nooks and crannies, but tonight, since the home did sit on the edge of town, she really felt alone. If someone tried to break in, no one would hear her screams.

Her only means of contact would be her cell phone.

She hurried back to the kitchen, leaving the living-room light on, the thud of her footsteps louder than she'd ever heard them before. The thought of eating nearly made her sick. Supper was not in her immediate future.

A quick rummage through her purse produced her phone. Clutching the device to her chest, Steph turned on even the small-wattage light over the kitchen sink, before hurrying to her room. She flicked on the overhead light, turned on the bedside lamp then headed to the bathroom, where she did the same with the last unlit fixture in her home.

She made a face at her reflection in the mirror. "This is so stupid."

If anyone was planning to break in, they already knew she was home alone. Lights wouldn't deter a dogged intruder. Still, they made her feel marginally better, and she wasn't about to turn a single one off.

Sleep? Maybe. Maybe not.

In a handful of minutes, she'd washed her face, brushed her teeth, debated whether to don pj's or stay fully clothed and shoed in case someone did try to break in, opted for the pj's and crawled into bed. Her fluffy down blanket felt as light as the feathers that filled it but would offer the warmth she'd craved since she'd stepped out of her store.

A second crawled by. Another…three dozen more.

What was going on? Why would someone ruin a number of products on her shelves? And who had tried to break in? She was sure the mugging had been an attempt to get inside the store.

Had it been a run-of-the-mill robber, he wouldn't have left her purse and the deposit pouch behind.

A car drove past on the road out of town, the hum of its engine and the splash of tires over the wet surface a frightening sound for the first time ever.

Steph scanned her bedroom, the cozy haven she'd made for herself. She'd only given her closet-romantic heart free rein in this room. A white-painted antique dresser sat at the right side of the window, while a wicker chair flanked the other side. The bed, also painted white, wore carved floral embel-lishments at the crest of the headboard, and she always piled it high with pillows and cushions, all of them decorated with embroidery, delicate vintage fabrics, ruffles, ribbons and lace. A white-on-white embroidered coverlet finished the bedding, and she'd always found the room soothing and welcoming.

But not tonight. Her safe little world had taken a blow. And she didn't know how to make things right once again.

Before she went off the deep end and gave her lively imag-ination the chance to run away with her common sense, Steph reached for her Bible. With experienced hands, she flipped through it to her favorite verse. She took a deep breath, and as always, read Jesus' words out loud.

"'I will never leave you; never will I forsake you.'"

No doubt about it. He was a clumsy oaf when it came to women.

Hal pulled into the driveway of the sturdy old home he'd bought last year. It was a comfortable place, with large rooms, beautiful wood floors and leaded windows, but it was also a lonely place. That's why he'd rescued a greyhound. Pepper was the best idea he'd ever had.

Maybe she was the only girl for him.

In college, he'd envied the guys with the smooth lines, but he hadn't been able to imitate them. The stuff they came up with had always felt so fake. Sure, he'd dated, but not often, regu-larly or for long. Plus, he'd never forgotten Steph Scott. Every girl he'd met had started out with that strike against her.

After today, seeing Steph's courage, her strength and her sweet gentleness, he was more certain than ever that all females he met always would.

Hal loped up to his front porch. On the other side of the

door, Pepper's nails tapped out an urgent SOS. She'd been locked in far longer than usual today.

As soon as he opened up, the sleek animal shot past him and straight to her favorite corner of the side yard, not ready to listen to his apology, not ready to forgive his slip. Then, when she trotted back inside, she graced Hal with a disdainful glare and shook herself within inches of his already soaked uniform pants' legs. Hal knew many pet owners believed their animals had human traits. But when it came to Pepper he didn't just believe it, he knew it.

She was uncannily human.

"All right, your royal highness." He chuckled as he headed for the tall aluminum trash can where he stored Pepper's kibble. "Forgive me, please! I am only a mere mortal and was detained by work."

Hal scooped out a healthy serving of the crunchy chunks.

Pepper sniffed, unwilling to even lick his hand, her usual form of love-filled greeting. She burrowed into her meal as if Hal weren't in the room.

He walked out of the former larder he'd turned into a first-floor laundry room, and then called back, "What're you going to do when I do land a date with Steph?"

Crunch, crunch, crunch.

Yeah, well. Maybe Pepper had it right, and he was dreaming. The way he'd acted at Steph's hadn't won him any awards. Suave, smooth and leading-man savvy, he wasn't. But he was a decent, hardworking Christian and even more attracted to Steph now than he had been back in school, or more recently, from a distance.

She'd blossomed into a lovely woman.

In the large living room, Hal turned on his stereo to a Charlotte classic jazz station. As the sassy sound of Dave

Brubeck's "Blue Rondo a la Turk" filled his home, Hal felt his energy return. He had paint to strip from molding upstairs, and Blue Rondo's beat should work to kick-start him into gear.

But before he made it to the stairs, his cell phone rang, and he had to turn down the sound. "Hello?"

"It's Maggie Lowe. Sorry to bother you in the evening, Hal, but the guys at the lab just called. They did lift some prints from the blood pressure cuff box. I figured since you'd responded twice to calls to the pharmacy, you'd be interested in what they found."

"Let me take a stab at it. You tell me how close I come. They found Steph's prints, those of the skinny kid who fills her shelves, and nothing else."

"We weren't surprised, either." Maggie fell silent for a moment. "Don't know what it means—or whether it means anything at all."

Hal sat in his wide leather armchair then propped his feet on the matching ottoman. "What's really important here is whether the mugger is connected with the…I don't know what to call Steph's vandal. But that's what I want to know."

"That is the question. And just so you know, we're going to drive around the pharmacy a little more often until we get this figured out."

Good. "We're sorta strapped for manpower—budgets, you know—but I'll get my deputies to make a couple of runs by the pharmacy a time or two a day."

"We appreciate the help. Two of our officers got new jobs, one in Atlanta and the other in Phoenix, during the summer. We're down to just Wayne and me, and we're looking to hire a pair of experienced cops. Well, we do have the chief, but you know his limitations."

"Bruce is a good man."

"But with tough limitations."

Bruce Zacharias had been one of Charlotte's best two decades ago, but these days his biggest battle was against worsening rheumatoid arthritis. He handled all of Loganton's administrative work, directed Maggie and Wayne and was rumored to be about to announce his retirement.

"We all have our limitations, Maggie. That's why I wish Steph had cameras in and around that store. They would catch what all of us, out of necessity and because of other assignments, miss."

Hal stared at the stacked logs in his fireplace. His home always gave him a great deal of satisfaction, but tonight, nothing seemed to ease the knot in his right shoulder or the one in his gut. Maybe it was just hunger. He'd picked up his dinner from Granny Annie's just as the woman was about to lock up.

Maybe it was Steph's situation.

"I think we'll get further on this one if we team up," he told the police officer. "I'm sure you guys want this stopped, and I don't want to see Steph Scott hurt again."

"10-4, Sheriff Benson, 10-4."

They hung up after brief good-nights, and then Hal went to ignite the pile of kindling he'd set out that morning before leaving for work. Soon, he had lively flames dancing in the fireplace, but instead of "Blue Rondo," he'd put a moody Miles Davis CD into the player. The woodwork could wait another day.

He zapped the meal, and at the microwave's ping, he took a fork, his plate and a glass of iced tea to his leather armchair. He began to eat his belated supper, not tasting a single bite.

If nothing else, he would keep Steph safe.

The next day, when Hal walked into Granny Annie's for lunch, he almost turned right around without even pausing for a drink. Just inside the door, he came face-to-face with Ed Townsend, the other contender for his job in the up-coming election.

The freshly minted lawyer had been giving Hal headaches with his legalese-laced diatribes, and Hal preferred to avoid meeting the man in public places. Ed never missed a chance to attack Hal.

"Well, hello there, Sheriff!" the red-haired lawyer cried in an overly hearty voice. "Had yourself a busy couple of days lately, I hear. I'm sure a law-and-order man like yourself has the culprits behind bars by now, right? Has Miss Scott's mugger been assigned a public defender? How about the vandal? Our Con-stitution does provide him with the right to legal representation, and everyone does have the right to due process, you know."

Hal fought the urge to grind his teeth—or grind Ed's teeth with five itching knuckles. "We're taking care of the matter, Ed. Now, if you'll excuse me—"

"Still *taking care* of the matter?" The lawyer's reddish mustache wriggled with ill-concealed glee. "You mean we still have a mugger loose in town?"

With a quick glance around the diner, Hal verified that every ear, if not eye, was glued to the conversation. "Sorry to deny you the pleasure," he told Ed. "But you know I can't discuss the particulars of an ongoing investigation. So if you don't mind, I'd like to order some lunch."

Ed opened his arms wide and spun to glance at everyone in the diner. "There you have it, folks. Your sheriff at his best. Lunch at Granny Annie's takes priority to investigating crime. *You* know who to vote for, who'll keep you safe." He winked at Hal. "See ya in the voting booth in November."

As Ed sauntered out and Hal's cheeks sizzled, Granny Annie barged through the swinging doors to the kitchen.

"What's the matter with that Townsend boy? He gets hisself a fancy paper from that there Duke University Law School, and he thinks he can go around blabbin' nonsense all day long."

Had there been any way to do so without ruining every last chance of winning reelection, Hal would have slunk right out of the diner. Public humiliation was not a meal a man swallowed easily.

And he didn't need five-foot-nothing Granny Annie to defend him. She might, however, make a spectacular campaign manager.

Then Mr. Cooper, the postmaster, stood up, slapped a bill into Granny's hand and shook his head. "That, folks, is why none of us is fool enough to vote for Ed."

Although it wasn't unanimous, Hal counted more nods than not. There was no way he could leave his county to Ed's questionable mercies. It was rumored the lawyer saw the sheriff's spot as a rung up the political ladder and nothing more. What kind of commitment was that? What kind of service would Ed provide?

Maybe he really should enlist Granny's help. She was the county's most efficient means of information proliferation, and he could stand all the positive talking-up he could get. In that regard, Granny might be an asset.

Then again, maybe not. She was also a dyed-in-the-wool matchmaker who made no secret she wanted nothing more than to find a match for Hal.

His cell phone rang. The LCD display showed his new deputy Patsy's number. He flicked it open, fully aware that, as comforting as her staunch support was, he couldn't let Granny's antics distract him. He had real crime to deal with.

He had Steph to protect.

And his job to save.

THREE

On Thursday, Steph noticed a significant increase in browser traffic through the store. At first, it irritated her. Then it amused her—after all, how many neighbors were going to miss the chance to check out the notorious blood pressure cuff boxes? On the other hand, she did wonder if they were just curious or if they expected to find a twenty sticking out of another box.

Darcy stopped by while on an errand for Miss Tabitha. "You're the talk of the town, girl!" She punctuated her words with a bubble-gum pop.

"Tell me about it."

"Don't knock it," Darcy said, chewing away. "Think of the increased cha-ching! Your bank account will love the craziness of it all."

"Give me normalcy—*please.*"

With a laugh, Darcy left. The constant flow of looky-loos continued.

Even Chad Adams hung around for an eternity after making his delivery—at least, he hung around long enough to locate the case of insulin syringes they had marked as missing from the delivery. Surprise, surprise! It turned up in his truck. At two o'clock Steph found him still wandering the aisles, a second bag of licorice in hand.

Chad could always use an extra twenty. The postmaster's younger brother-in-law had a streak of failed ventures under his belt and a list of worthless patents to his name. Mr. Cooper often complained about Chad's mooching ways.

At a quarter to four, Jimmy came up to the pharmacy counter to complain about the many times in the forty-five minutes since he'd come to work he'd had to mop the entry because of all the muddy footprints. Steph gave in to the inevitable. She laughed.

"Let it go for a while," she told the teen. "We're today's talk of the town. They're going to keep coming, so you may as well wait until later to clean up the mess. Just be glad it's no longer raining. The mud will dry up out there soon enough."

The boy shrugged. "If you say so. I just hope nobody trips and falls checking out those boxes."

"Tell you what," she said. "I have a new mat in the back room. Why don't you bring it out? At least we can offer a dry one to any customer who comes in between now and closing time."

Jimmy trudged off, muttering something about the waste of a perfectly good mat.

Mat or no mat, Steph kept a close eye on everyone who wandered through the store. It took some work, but she refused to let down her guard. She would do whatever it took to protect the business for which she'd worked so hard. She wasn't going to let some petty vandal or back-alley mugger damage her professional image. She would not let a criminal intimidate her.

For the first time in the five years since she'd opened the store, Steph felt stressed. It usually didn't matter how busy she was; what mattered was serving her customers. But with all the gawkers who'd streamed in that day, Steph just wanted the clock's hands to move a little faster.

And for the town of Loganton to find a new fixation.

On Friday at a quarter to six, after another day of town curiosity, the bell on the door clanged yet again. When Steph glanced up from the prescription she'd been filling, her gaze snagged on Hal Benson's warm brown eyes. He took his time walking through the store, strolling up and down the aisles, checking out the items on the shelves.

"Need anything you can't find?" she asked when he reached her counter.

"Just getting acquainted with the areas I don't frequent. And I wanted to see where you keep your blood pressure cuffs."

Steph capped the orange pill bottle and stuck the computerized label in place before looking back up. "You do realize the cuff's only the last item damaged in a rash of six."

"Tell me about the damaged items. And what the damage looked like."

"We can start with the box of tissues. The glued flaps on one side of the box had been sliced open—neatly and with some sharp object. A knife, probably. It couldn't have happened during shipping. It was no accident. On the other hand, the tissues themselves were crumpled and some even torn."

"What do you mean by crumpled?"

"That was the strangest part. The flaps hung open outward, but the tissues were smashed inward."

"Pushed in."

"That's right."

"What else?"

Steph caught a glimpse of the clock on the pharmacy wall. "Tell you what, Sheriff—"

"If you're just Steph, then I'm just Hal."

She smiled, remembering his shyness the night before.

"Okay, Hal. It's almost six, and I need to close the store. If you'll give me a few minutes so I can focus on the details, then I'll tell you everything I remember."

"That'll work."

As Steph picked up her ledger, she noticed the intent expression on the sheriff's face. "Is something wrong?"

"Wrong? No, nothing's wrong. I was just thinking...since you still have work to do here, how about you finish up, and then, maybe...well, if you don't have anything else going on, maybe we can stop at Granny Annie's—for a cup of coffee, you know? You can tell me all about the other damaged items then."

Had he just asked her out on a strange kind of date? Or was the sheriff so shy he couldn't even ask a woman to discuss evidence over a cup of coffee at Granny Annie's Diner?

"Sounds great," she said. "And just the thought of a slice of one of Granny's pies is enough to spur me through my routine."

His relief was almost palpable. "Terrific! You don't mind if I wait here for you, do you? I don't want you to have to go out into the alley alone. You never know if the mugger might come back."

Steph shuddered. She hadn't thought about that. But now that Hal had mentioned the alley, she didn't like the idea of going outside, in the dark, by herself. "I don't mind. On the contrary, I appreciate your offer. I won't be long. I just have to double-check the prescriptions I filled today to keep track of what goes out."

"You can't be too careful about that kind of thing."

"That's what I think."

She eased away from the counter, matched the day's spreadsheet on her computer screen to the list in the ledger, counted the empty pill bottles in their bin, checked that number against yesterday's count and smiled when the numbers added up. Most pharmacists wouldn't go through so much trouble, but she always feared a distraction during her busy day might rouse her ADD and lead to a mistake.

With one tug, the grate over the pharmacy-counter window clanged into place, and once she'd locked it, Steph ducked down to pick up the deposit pouch from under her desk. Moments later, it bulged with the cash, checks and credit slips she cleared from the register tray. Her evening routine had become so automatic to her that she sometimes had to stop herself and think through all the steps to make sure she'd done everything before she walked away.

Sweater and purse in hand, she locked up. "I'm done."

And there he was, standing in the small hallway that led to the back door. Once again, it struck Steph how tall he was. Lean and lanky, Hal Benson had to stand at least six foot three inches tall. And he looked hewn from taut, ropy muscle, too. There was something very comforting about his size and quiet, serious demeanor. It didn't hurt that Hal's craggy features reminded her of the heroes in the classic Western movies she'd watched growing up.

When he took her elbow to guide her out the door, Steph felt safe and protected. "Thanks."

"What for?"

"For realizing I'd be scared well before it occurred to me."

As she opened the back door, he reached over her head to hold it open for her. "I suspect you would have been fine. Don't forget. The mugger didn't try to get inside last night. But since things seem quiet around the county tonight, and I do want to know what you remember about the other incidents of vandalism…" He shrugged.

The sheriff waited until she'd started her car before he headed toward his cruiser. The drive to Granny Annie's didn't take long, for which Steph was thankful, since she didn't want to analyze her feelings about their maybe date, maybe interrogation outing to Loganton's gossip hub. By tomorrow morning, everyone in town would know she'd had coffee with the single and attractive county sheriff.

Half would insist they were Loganton's latest version of Sleeping Beauty and Prince Charming, the other half that she was headed for jail.

Steph pulled into the parking lot behind the diner. She threw on her sweater, since the weather had grown considerably chillier when the sun began to slide down to the horizon, and then hurried toward the diner's door.

Halfway there, a sound startled her. She stopped, listened, eyes flicking from corner to corner, to her car, the street out front, the back door of the diner. She saw no one anywhere near. Her stomach muscles tightened. Had those been footsteps she'd heard? Had Hal arrived?

Even though she strained to hear, she only managed to pick up the hiss of the fall breeze through the trees on Main Street. And the galloping beat of her heart. For a moment, she felt discouraged. Nervousness had never been a problem, and Steph resented what the mugger had done to her. The thought of spending the rest of her life with an ear cocked to potential and possibly imagined danger held no appeal. She wanted her peaceful life back. That peace was one of the reasons she'd come home to Loganton after earning her pharmacy license.

She took a step toward the diner, hesitated, unsure of what to do. Should she go in and get a booth, or should she wait for Hal? If she waited, aside from freezing, would she also make herself bait for the mugger? Had there been someone out here following her? Or had her mind started to play tricks on her?

A car turned the corner. Relief flooded her when she caught sight of the county seal on the driver door: the sheriff's cruiser. Steph exhaled as she ran up the diner's front steps.

Inside the fragrant eatery, she went straight for the last empty booth, smiling a greeting to everyone who called out a hello. A glance out the window as she slid all the way in on the slick vinyl showed Hal striding toward the diner, that confident pace of his eating up the distance. More greetings rang out when he walked in.

"Can you believe this weather? First a monsoon, and now it's fit to freeze off your cat's whiskers," Granny Annie called out from behind the counter. "Karla, girl! Get Miss Steph and the sheriff some hot coffee. We gotta warm 'em up quick. It's cold and getting colder out there tonight."

The sassy senior ducked out of sight then popped back up. She stared out the front windows and shook her head. "Can you believe it's only six thirty?" she asked. "It's getting dark so early…it looks more like nine or ten o'clock."

Hal tapped his uniform hat against the side of the table to dislodge the drops beaded on its surface. He darted a glance at Steph. "My stomach's very accurate clock says it's just about supper time. Want to join me? For more than just coffee, I mean."

The scent of roasted meat, stewed tomatoes and something cinnamony for dessert proved a temptation Steph didn't bother to resist. Moments later, when Karla skidded a pair of stoneware mugs full of steaming java across their table, she asked the young waitress, "What does Granny have tonight?"

Karla cocked a hip and pulled the pencil out from its perch behind her ear. "She's got meat loaf, mashed potatoes and gravy, buttered corn and biscuits, and the other choice is chicken-fried steak with cream gravy, hash brown casserole, stewed tomatoes and corn bread."

Steph's mouth watered. "Bring me the steak, please."

"I'll have the meat loaf," Hal said.

"And a side of cholesterol meds in our future," Steph added with a grin when Karla had sauntered off. "But every once in a while, you just have to go for the comfort food. Tonight's the perfect night for it."

The sheriff's warm gaze paused on her face. "After what you went through the past two days, I'm not surprised you're looking for comfort."

Steph studied the foil lid on the tiny container of cream. "I'll admit it's rattled me. I went right to bed after you left last night."

The sheriff frowned as he whipped a notepad and pen from his uniform pocket. "Let's get to work then. I want this guy off my streets."

Hal listened as Steph described the damaged goods. Every so often, he wrote down a detail, his attention on her every word. She described the tissue box again, the box of disposable diapers, the boxed twelve-pack of nutritional supplement shakes, the vaporizer box and the box of cotton balls.

"As far as I can tell," she said when she couldn't think of anything else, "the only thing those items have in common is that they all came packed in cardboard boxes and were carefully cut."

The sheriff took a swig of his black coffee. "I noticed that. Now I just have to figure out how all those boxes relate to each other."

Karla arrived with a heavy tray with two platter-size plates just as overloaded. The mountain of hash browns laced with cheddar and sour cream on Steph's dish gave off tendrils of steam. Creamy gravy dotted with pepper flakes dressed the battered and deep-fried steak. The side bowl of tangy stewed tomatoes had Steph reaching for her napkin then spreading it over her lap.

She laced her hands over the napkin, prayed silently and was pleased to hear Hal say, "Amen."

They looked up and their gazes held. He smiled. "Don't let it get cold. Granny's meals are best when they're hot."

"Hey, Sheriff!" Granny Annie called. "It's about time you didn't come eat your supper alone. Make a habit of it, you hear?"

With her fork a mere inch from her mouth, Steph stole a glance at her dining companion. Just like last night and earlier today in the store, a hint of a blush reddened his cheeks. For some reason, that small detail endeared the serious sheriff to her.

"One of these days," he muttered, "she'll learn the meaning of tact."

Steph chuckled. "Don't count on it. She's been embarrassing folks in Loganton for a generation or two."

His sheepish grin only made her laugh again. It was the first time she'd laughed since the senior citizens had left Scott's the day before. It felt great.

Hal leaned closer. "Let's eat before she comes out here and pulls our ears," he said in a loud stage whisper.

Twenty minutes later, Steph put down the dessert spoon as she savored the last mouthful of peach cobbler. She leaned back, stuffed but satisfied. "I just remembered why I don't eat like this too often."

"Unfortunately, I do. One of these days, I'm going to get around to cracking open the covers of that cookbook I bought last summer after I moved into the house. I have to learn to cook. I'll miss Granny Annie's meals, but my health sure won't—"

The crackle of a walkie-talkie cut off his words. "Sheriff Hal?" a woman's soprano asked.

Hal brought the black device up to his mouth. "What's up?"

"I know you're on a break, and you're probably having

dinner, but we just got a DUI out on the old River Run Road. Sounds pretty bad. Will called in and asked for backup."

"Got it. I'm on my way."

"10-4, Sheriff. And thanks."

Hal slid out of the booth, then reached for his wallet. "I'm sorry. Duty calls. Please stay and enjoy another cup of Granny's coffee on me."

She shook her head and followed him, unwilling to linger without him. Before Steph's fingers unzipped her purse, Hal had dropped a couple of bills on the counter by the register. "Keep the change, Karla. Put it toward college."

The teen grinned, rang them up and handed Hal a receipt.

"Thanks," Steph said as they reached the door. So it had been part date, part interrogation, as she'd thought. "Don't apologize. I understand. Besides, I didn't sleep well last night. I hope to do better tonight."

He opened the door. "Keep your cell phone close."

Steph pulled her sweater tight across her chest. "I kept it under my pillow last night, and I plan to do the same until…well, you understand."

As she splashed to her car, she thanked the Lord for Hal's company and his heavy steps behind her. This time, Steph didn't have to wonder. She wasn't alone, and she knew as long as Hal was around he'd keep her safe.

At home, she knew she could count on the Lord.

On Saturday morning, when the rain and the damp chill were only memories, Steph sang along to a MercyMe CD in the car's stereo on her way to work. She parked at her normal spot in the parking lot across the alley then opened up the store. Jimmy was waiting at the front door.

"'Morning, Miss Steph. No more mopping, huh?"

"Not today," she called over her shoulder on her way to open the pharmacy itself. "As long as you sweep in front of the door, we'll be fine."

Then she reached the white-painted steel door. The *open* white pharmacy door. Steph stared in disbelief.

She remembered locking up the night before. That's when she'd turned and nearly bumped into Hal. She *had* closed and locked that door.

Hadn't she?

A chill ran through her. A vise of tension wound itself around her head. Her heart beat louder, and her breath came in short spurts. Nausea seared up her chest and into her throat.

"Easy," she murmured. No reason to freak out. Not yet.

Careful not to let her fingers touch anything, Steph kneed the door ajar. She slipped inside and headed for the cabinet where she kept the narcotics behind yet another lock. But before she got there, she caught sight of the empty shelf against the back wall.

The pseudoephedrine was gone. Her worst nightmare had come to pass. The thief was making meth.

Steph reached for her cell phone and dialed 911.

FOUR

Steph forced her fingers to relax. She'd laced them to keep the shaking to a minimum, but as Officer Donnelly's questions continued to come at her, they'd tightened to where the knuckles had turned white.

"What more can I tell you?" she asked, exhausted by the events of the past few days. "I didn't see anything. And I doubt Jimmy saw anything, either. We walked in together. He headed to the back room to hang up his jacket, while I went toward the pharmacy counter. That's when I found the door…and the pseudoephedrine…"

And her nightmare began all over again. Or got worse. In either case, Steph felt besieged. One thing after the other after the other. She hated the expressions on the police officers' faces. They didn't bother to hide the skepticism on top of their whopping dollops of disbelief. That disbelief bothered her the most. Did they really think she'd be so careless as to leave the pharmacy unlocked?

She wasn't negligent. ADD or no ADD, she took her responsibilities seriously.

The bell on the front door rang out. Great. She should have thought to hang up the CLOSED sign when the questions started. But she hadn't thought of much beyond the missing drugs.

She glanced up to see who'd come in. An involuntary smile erupted. She couldn't quite put a finger on the reason why, but just the sight of Hal Benson brightened her dreary outlook.

He nodded toward the two officers but kept his warm brown-eyed gaze on her. "Everyone okay here?"

She nodded. "The pharmacy door's the only casualty."

While Officer Donnelly brought the sheriff up to speed, Steph thought back over everything that had happened. Nothing stood out. But something did occur to her.

"Someone's been watching me," she said.

The three law enforcement officers faced her.

"Whoever knocked me off the back steps didn't give up. Even though he didn't get the key the first time, he came back last night. And that's when he succeeded getting in. The question I have for you—" all three looked surprised "—is how did he get in? You know and I know he never got that key."

Hal's cheeks turned a touch ruddy. "Before I came inside I went to take a quick look at that back door. I didn't spend a whole lot of time checking, but I think your thief had a key. There was no obvious evidence of tampering."

Steph shook her head. "I have the only key to that lock. I had all new locks installed before I opened for business."

He rubbed the side of his nose with a long index finger. "Then he must have had a master key or had someone make a copy. We'll need to contact locksmiths."

"What about the front door?" she asked. "Did you check that lock?"

The sheriff's brown eyes flicked toward the front of the store. He shook his head. "It's too visible. Anyone driving by would have seen someone—not you, since you at your own door wouldn't raise any suspicion—unlocking the door in the middle of the night…or early in the morning."

His gaze flew around the store. "You didn't get a chance to do anything about those security cameras, did you?"

"When would I have had the time?"

"Too bad. The cameras might have given us something concrete to go on. You do need to get them. And don't put it off."

As if she could afford such pricey measures. But it looked like she wasn't going to have a choice in the matter. "I'll look into the cameras."

A steady pounding started in her temple. Steph rubbed, wishing she could eliminate it that easily. Who could it have been? She knew just about everyone in town and couldn't begin to see any of her neighbors playing the part of drug thief.

Appearances could be deceiving, but this went further.

Someone must be living a double life, one that endangered the lives of others, especially those of vulnerable, hurting folks. And kids. That, she took personally.

"We have to stop this," she said, her voice almost a whisper, but steely in conviction. "I was so happy when I heard the meth lab had been burned down. Especially since the guy behind it was caught and locked up. But I guess it's true what they say. Where one is picked up, two or more pop up to take his place."

A warm hand landed on her shoulder. "That's the reality of the drug trade," Hal said. "It's always something like ten steps ahead of us, no matter how hard we try."

"Then we just have to start moving faster and smarter, with no time for breaks," she countered. "Especially for the sake of the kids. We have to protect them."

"First, Miss Scott," Officer Donnelly said, "we have to catch us a thief. Is there anything else you can tell us? Anything at all?"

Steph closed her eyes, tried to picture the moments before

she made the horrible discovery and then shook her head. "Honestly, I've told you everything I can remember. Was Jimmy able to help you? Did he see anything I might have missed?"

Maggie Lowe shook her head. "I sent him home right before I came back in here. He knew even less than you."

"And you found nothing, *nothing* to go on?"

Hal shrugged. "I want to take a closer look out there before I leave. But my quick check didn't find anything that caught my eye."

She sighed. "Then if that's all, could we please finish? I'd like to close up and go home. I don't think I've ever been so tired in my whole life."

The two officers traded looks. "I suppose we can go now," Officer Donnelly said, reluctance in his voice and on his heavy features. "We know where you live, and I'm sure you'll understand if we have to check with you some more."

She gave the man a wry smile. "Is that the new version of 'Don't leave town'?"

The senior officer tightened his lips and gave her a disapproving look. "I wouldn't be joking at a time like this, Miss Scott."

Steph bit down on her tongue to keep from making any kind of comment. She wasn't usually the kind to mouth off, but she'd thought she was bringing levity into an awful situation. Evidently, it was even more awful than she thought. The cops couldn't make themselves smile.

She watched the two officers leave, a sense of failure lodged in her heart. Then she noticed Hal Benson taking a slow, methodic stroll up and down the pharmacy aisles, stopping every few steps to scour the shelves. When he finished his circle and came back to her side, she stood. He was so tall.

"Any more damaged goods?" he asked.

"Nothing we've found."

He gave a brief nod. "You will keep your eye out for anything unusual, won't you?"

"You are kidding, aren't you? After everything that's happened, I'm going to be like an eagle. This store is my baby. I won't let some miserable criminal ruin everything I've worked so hard to accomplish. Besides, the town needs my services. I'm the only pharmacist for miles."

She thought she saw a flash of admiration brighten the sheriff's expression before he again donned his neutral look. "I'm sorry this is happening to you," he added. "And I'm afraid there'll be more to come. Now that the pseudoephedrine was stolen, you realize the pharmacy board will have to get involved."

His words hit her almost as hard as a slug to her gut. She shook her head, hoping against hope. "This is a criminal matter, not a professional one. Someone broke in and robbed me. I wasn't negligent. I don't see why they would start an investigation against me. I've done nothing wrong."

"Didn't suggest you had, but because the meth problem has grown so huge these days, we've begun to work with them, so we let them know whenever something happens. They'll likely have questions for you, if not a full-fledged investigation."

The last thing she wanted was a strike against her, especially since December wasn't that far away. She had to file for license renewal by the first. It expired at the end of the year; all North Carolina pharmacy licenses did. Just to think her license—her pharmacy itself—might be in jeopardy because of a thief was more than she could handle.

"Go ahead," Hal said. "Lock up. I'll wait until you're ready to leave to yellow-tape the place. I might even follow you home, even though it's only early afternoon."

Steph blushed. "I'm sorry. But you don't have to babysit

me. I'll be fine. I'm sure you have better things to do with your Saturday afternoon."

He barked out a chuckle. "Only if you ask my dog. Pepper's convinced she's the center of the universe."

"You're not on duty?"

"Even a sheriff gets a day off."

"Now I'm really sorry. You didn't have to come out for this. I'm sure the officers did fine and would have without you. Really, go home. I'm sure you'll have a better time with Pepper than hanging around this place while I do my obsessive thing and close up."

"I watched you last night, but I wasn't paying that close attention to your routine. I'd like to watch again. Maybe there's something you missed—"

"I've been doing the same thing for five years now, Sheriff Benson. I'll have you know, it's become like breathing for me. The same steps every single night—do you understand?" At his nod, she went on. "This matters. It's critically important. Lives are at stake. I don't take my work lightly."

He held his hands out as if to ward off further attack. "But anyone can make a mistake. I didn't mean anything by my comment. Besides, I might have missed something when you closed up. I already said I wasn't paying that close attention last night."

"You might have missed something, but *I* didn't miss a step," she said, her voice tight. "You're certainly welcome to watch."

It was hard to ignore his presence; a six-foot-plus man acting like a shadow wasn't easily ignored. But Steph focused on her routine, and while there was no pseudoephedrine to check on behind the counter, she still went through the motions. Once she was done, she went out the back door, but just as she was about to slip the key into the lock, Hal stopped her.

"Hang on." He dropped to one knee and peered at the lock from just a few inches away, his eyes narrowed, a pair of lines between his brows. After a few intense minutes, he murmured a vague "Hmm…"

"Well?" she asked, her heart beating like a relentless jackhammer. The pain in her temples intensified. "What did you find?"

"Not a whole lot of anything, but it is gray and sticky. Someone might have made a wax or maybe a clay cast of the lock."

"Is that how someone would have a new key made?"

"That's one way." He reached for his cell phone. "Give me a few minutes while I get Donnelly and Lowe back out here. They need to collect this stuff off the lock."

Half of her was tempted to wait for him. The other half felt relief. She now had the perfect way to leave him behind. She didn't want him to see how upset she really was. "Don't worry about me. I'll be fine. I'm heading straight home, and the Farmer's Supply is still open. Nothing's going to happen when that many people are only feet away from my front door."

The sheriff didn't look happy, but Officer Donnelly answered the call just then. Steph waved and headed toward her car. How she managed to get home without hitting another vehicle would forever remain a mystery. The only thing her mind would entertain was the memory of the open pharmacy door and the empty shelf…the feel of the thief shoving her from the steps…the sinking sensation in her stomach when Jimmy had brought her the blood pressure cuff box.

At home, she pulled into the garage, turned off the engine, clicked the automatic door opener and then, once its whir died away, trudged up the stairs. She supposed she should boot up her laptop and look into purchasing those surveillance cameras, but she didn't feel she could concentrate right then.

She dropped her purse on her bistro table and then poured a glass of iced tea. Feeling more tired than she should have, since it was only early afternoon, she decided to lie down for a while.

Moisture beaded the outside of her glass. It would mark the top of the nightstand, but Steph couldn't make herself move to go find a coaster. The fear and stress of the past few days had finally taken over. What if she was refused renewal of her license? What if the police became convinced she'd had something to do with the theft? What if she lost everything she'd worked so hard to achieve?

She'd fought so hard to overcome the ADD all through school and college. It had taken what always felt like superhuman effort to finish her education and establish herself as a dependable professional.

All that time, kids and teachers had seen her as a spacey daydreamer because of her learning disability. She didn't blame them. She had been spacey, and even these days, she still spent a fair amount of time daydreaming. But that wasn't the only way to view her.

She'd been blessed with an opportunity to work with a counselor who specialized in ADD while in college. With the kind woman's help, Steph had learned how to establish systems and parameters for herself, and staying within them had allowed her to succeed.

The ability to support herself, as well as the chance to run a thriving business in her hometown, mattered to her. It was especially important since the town had lost a number of other businesses over the past few years. She loved Loganton. She didn't want it to die.

But now…now she might fail.

A tear slid out the corner of her eye and rolled down into her hair. She lay on her back, immobile, fighting the sense of defeat that hovered above her. At that moment, her faith, the certainty in the Lord that had always carried her through the worst of times, seemed weak and far from her grasp.

She blinked away more tears, and in doing so, caught sight of the delicate lace curtains on her window. How silly could a grown woman get? She should have outgrown the romantic fantasies of her teenage years by now.

But it didn't matter how silly it might seem to others. Deep in her heart, Steph knew a great deal of the dreamy teen remained. If she were to be brutally honest with herself, which she tried to be, she would admit she still hoped for a hero, one who would romance her with all the flowers, intimate dinners and whispered words of love she'd imagined all those years ago. True, she'd only let that part of her have free rein there in her bedroom, but she was unwilling to let anyone think she was still the flighty girl she'd once been.

The Song of Solomon told her God didn't deny the opportunity for romance in a believer's life. So she kept that part of her hidden, only for God and her to know about.

Sure, she was waiting for her hero. But in the meantime, she could fully focus on her business. Her dreams didn't interfere with her work. She couldn't stand the thought that her customers might come to mistrust her. What else did a pharmacist have but that confidence on the part of those who depended on her for their health?

Brrrring!

For a moment, she thought of ignoring the phone. But because of the kind of work she did, and because she was the only pharmacist in the area, she didn't dare. Someone might need a prescription filled in a hurry.

"Hello?"

"Are you okay?" Darcy Thomas, her best friend, asked.

"You heard? Already?"

Darcy popped her bubble gum. "Hey, we live in the gossip capital of the world. So are you going to tell me about what happened?"

"You know what, Darce? I don't really feel like talking about it right now."

A silent beat. Then, "So are you ready?"

"Ready for what?"

Another pause. "I can't believe you forgot. You're the one who said she needed a new pair of shoes. I'm just going along for the ride. Did the Beast rise up and steal your memory again?"

A vague wisp of remembrance teased the back of her mind. "Hmm…maybe I did. But after the week I've had, I don't think this has anything to do with the Beast." She and Darcy had named her learning disability years ago. "Shopping for shoes does sound okay though. Are you at the mall already?"

"No, I thought we could drive out together. With the cost of gas what it is these days, there's no reason to use both cars. Tell you what. Since you've had a rough time, I'll do the honors. Just be ready to run down in five."

Considering the condition of Darcy's finances, Steph couldn't let her do that. "Let me drive. It'll do me good. Kind of clean out those creepy spiders hanging out on the cobwebs in my head. Give me ten minutes, and I'll pick you up."

Darcy's silence made Steph think she'd turn down the offer, but then Darcy sighed. "I'm going to take you up on that. I'm way sore. Miss Tabitha's had me running up to the attic to bring down winter stuff all week, and one time I fell down that scrawny pull-down ladder thing."

The two friends said a quick goodbye. Steph rose and ran a brush through her hair, slicked on some rosy lip gloss, straightened her dark gold knit top and slipped her feet into her favorite brown leather flats. They were looking pretty ratty. It was time to find a replacement pair and put these out to pasture.

At least they'd be traveling in a car that would get them to the mall. Steph's best pal drove a beat-up old heap, and neither one of the two women was in any shape or mood to wind up on the side of the road waiting until a tow truck showed up to get the heap back to Loganton.

She was glad Darcy had called when she did. God had blessed her with their close friendship. While she hadn't wanted to do anything more than crawl under her sheets and nurse her wounds, she knew she'd be better off with the distraction the shopping safari would provide.

Before too long, she'd be telling Darcy every last detail of the trouble she'd faced since Wednesday. And Darcy would listen, offer comfort and by the time she came back home, Steph knew she'd be ready to tackle anything the world threw her way.

As she ran down to the garage, she felt her spirits rebounding; her optimism returned. They'd catch the thief. The sheriff struck her as a dog-with-a-bone kind of man, and she knew from way back how smart he really was. She could trust the man.

Eight minutes later, Steph pulled up to Darcy's place. They drove to the mall, and before long, they were busy comparing prices, styles, and laughing as though nothing unusual had happened. Over milk shakes in the food court, Steph told her friend about the break-in at Scott's.

"I'm so sorry," Darcy said, her voice serious, her expression concerned. "I wish this wasn't happening to you."

"Goes to show all those newscasters are right. Crime is on the rise everywhere." Steph took a last pull on her straw then stood. "Enough of this. Let's go look at shoes."

At their favorite shoe store, Steph found a pair of comfortable brown leather flats that wouldn't break the bank. Then, box tucked under her arm, she went looking for Darcy. She found her friend staring at a pair of sandals on clearance with longing in her eyes.

"Go ahead," she said. "They're a steal."

Darcy clamped her lips momentarily then shook her head. "No can do. The well's run dry this month. Maybe if they're still here after I get my next paycheck…"

Eight dollars and ninety-nine cents? Darcy couldn't afford a nine-dollar pair of sandals? A pang of sadness struck Steph. And she realized things weren't _so bad for her. True, she didn't have money to spend without thought, but she always paid her bills and could still afford to treat herself every so often. She even had a savings account—nothing impressive, but it grew a little each month.

What could she do? Would Darcy let her buy the shoes for her?

Steph glanced at her friend, who then squared her shoulders and headed for the cash register.

"What did you find?" Darcy asked.

For a moment, she thought of putting the shoes back on the seat where she'd tried them on then leaving the store. But that wouldn't help either one of them. What? What could she do?

As the clerk rang up her purchase, Steph thought and thought. But it wasn't until they were headed back to her car that anything occurred to her.

But how could she approach Darcy without offending her?

She offered up a quick prayer for the right words and launched her plea. "With everything as crazy as it's been at the store, it's looking ragged at the edges. I haven't had a chance to clean it as it should be cleaned. And Jimmy's only good for the occasional mopping after he sweeps the area by the door. I wish I had someone to take care of the cleaning."

Steph kept her gaze fixed on the car, but out the corner of her eye, she caught Darcy's sharp glance. As her friend let silent gum-chewing seconds go by, she began to doubt herself. She shouldn't have spoken up, she shouldn't have said a thing—

"Do you really have the money to pay someone?" Darcy asked, her voice tentative.

"You know I'm not rolling in dough, but I can take care of myself and the store. It will only be minimum wage, but it can help someone who needs the extra funds."

At the car door, Steph made a production of digging in her purse for the key. When she found it, she clicked the unlock button then said, "Would you be interested in something like that? I'm not sure I want to trust a stranger in the store, but you'd be a great help. After you're done at Miss Tabitha's, you understand."

Again, Darcy gave her a piercing look. "Only if you really need the help. I refuse charity—"

"I really need the help. How about you meet me at the store at six on Mondays, Fridays and Saturdays. Wednesdays you're already there helping me with the seniors."

Darcy blew a bubble. "Are you sure about this?"

"I'm absolutely sure."

Steph wanted to push, but she knew that was the quickest way to scare off her friend. She had to wait for Darcy to come around. It didn't take long.

"Do you need me tonight?" she finally said.

"No. The cops won't be taking down the yellow tape until sometime late tonight or tomorrow. Let's start on Monday."

"You got a deal."

Thank you, Lord! "We got a deal."

Feeling better than she had in days, Steph drove Darcy home. Now if they could just catch the thief, she'd be doing great.

As soon as he walked into the church sanctuary on Sunday morning, Hal found himself looking around for a particular blond head. Steph usually sat on the right side of the sanctuary and more often than not, with Darcy Thomas, even after all these years. He remembered the two of them giggling down the halls in school. They probably did less giggling these days, but the two women had clearly remained close over time.

He wished Steph could see in him as good a confidant as in Darcy. Maybe once this business at the pharmacy was resolved she would. He was determined to get to the bottom of the theft and the mugging. And the vandalism, too.

Wayne and Maggie had their suspicions about her. He didn't. He knew Steph couldn't have had anything to do with the theft.

He loved digging out the truth; he loved his job. He knew Steph loved what she did, too. It meant the world to him to help her keep on doing what she did so well.

As the first rich notes of the organ swelled to fill the old church, Hal bowed his head and prayed for wisdom and discernment. He was going to need an extra helping of both to help Steph. Aside from a couple of tiny crumbs of femo clay, they had nothing with which to build a case.

The worship, as always, filled him with joy. He loved the Lord. He had since as far back as he could remember. Pastor Art Reams's sermon made him think. The man of God had chosen to preach on John 10:10: "I have come that they may have life, and have it to the full."

What did it mean to live? To live for Christ? To follow the Savior? To answer His call?

For Art, it meant to feed His sheep's hungry spirits. For Hal, it meant to protect the sheep's vulnerable bodies, the things God had entrusted to them, and to try to keep the peace that unbelievers—and some troubled believers, too—so often sought to destroy.

At the end of the teaching, he stood with the rest of the congregation to join in the singing of his favorite hymn, the classic "How Great Thou Art." With a heart full of devotion, and determined to answer the call God had placed upon him, he headed out the door, hoping to catch Steph before she left.

Instead of finding Steph, he stumbled into Ed's path. The lawyer's black eyes sparkled when he saw Hal. "Well, good morning, Sheriff. How's our lovely county this fine day?"

For the first time that morning, Hal's shirt collar felt tight. He ran a finger between the stiff cotton and his vulnerable neck. "Seems fine to me."

When Ed glanced at the parking lot full of worshippers, Hal knew he'd been had.

"Then that must mean you caught the thief who stole the drugs from Scott's Pharmacy," the sheriff wannabe said, his smile smarmy, his tone of voice sly. "I'm glad to hear you got that poison off our streets right in time."

By then, every ear was attuned to the flamboyant man. Hal hated being the center of everyone's attention. Ed knew it. He also, too obviously, knew Hal hadn't caught the thief or secured the stolen drugs.

"We're on it, Counselor. We're on it."

"You're on it," the man said, his voice growing louder by the word, "but not done with it? Is that right, *Sheriff?*"

Taking a step toward his car, Hal nodded. "It's under control."

Ed faced the worshippers and their cars, arms spread wide. "Well, folks. I'd think y'all want a sheriff who'd have the case solved, the crook locked up and the drugs where they couldn't do your kiddies any harm. Give me your vote, and I'll see that's what you get."

His cheeks flaming, his stomach churning and his conscience reminding him to love his enemy, Hal nodded a farewell and kept walking toward his car.

But then, when he was just a few feet from his goal, he caught a scrap of conversation that chilled him to the bone.

Constance Moore, a relative newcomer to town, had a distinctive, husky voice that never failed to carry. "…Maybe that lawyer has a point about the sheriff. He's not moving so fast, if you ask me. But you know? I don't think the lawyer would be much better. I hear we have a retired Drug Enforcement Agency man in town these days, that he's settling down with a local girl. It would seem he's the one who should take over the job. Maybe we ought to start a write-in campaign…"

Hal had nothing against Ethan Rodgers. He personally liked the man, respected the years of service he'd given and admired the way the retired agent had brought a drug dealer to justice a few months earlier.

But…

But *he,* Hal Benson, was the sheriff, the right man for the job. Not Ethan. He knew what he was doing. Besides, Ethan was still recovering from wounds he'd sustained during the final confrontation with the dealer. Hal was ready, willing and able to serve.

And called to do so.

The last thing he needed was another contender, this one able to succeed on the job, experienced and competent. As he stuck the key in the ignition, he turned to his Lord. "Father, give me the strength I'll need for the battle to come. Can't do it without You, and I know it."

He pulled out into the after-church traffic, and it occurred to him he didn't know which of the two battles he'd wage first, since it was only too clear he faced two wars. One to keep his job, and the other to save Steph's.

It seemed they might really have to join forces and become the partners he'd suggested if they were to have any hope of winning either one.

He prayed his motives for the partnership were right. His disappointment was undeniable. This wasn't the time to romance Steph Scott. It was the time to serve her, the pharmacist, one of the citizens he was called to protect.

Not just the woman who'd fascinated him for so long, the one he could so easily come to love.

FIVE

Steph drove to Granny Annie's after the service. Ed's vicious campaigning had stunned her. From what she knew of the brand-new lawyer, he had no room to criticize Hal. Ed had trudged off to law school only after he'd sunk three consecutive businesses and burned through the fuel that funded his ventures. Now he seemed more than ready to use taxpayer dollars to float future ideas. Hopefully voters would prevent that.

At least he stood a chance of making a go of it as a lawyer. He certainly liked to hear himself talk. From the few attorneys she'd met, Steph knew that was one characteristic most of the successful ones shared. But law enforcement? *Ed?*

No way.

And to think he'd humiliated Hal like that. While she'd seen a handful of the congregants send measuring glances Hal's way after Ed's efforts, the majority had turned away in disgust—disgust with Ed, not Hal.

True, she didn't know a thing about catching crooks or arresting lawbreakers, but she did know she didn't trust Ed with either job. On the other hand, she believed Hal, because of the boy he'd been and the man he'd become, would excel where Ed would fail.

She parked and, with her purse slung over her shoulder, strolled to the diner, relishing the fall sunlight. She was more than sick of the rain that week. She had a sneaky suspicion she'd remember the mugging and the break-in every time it rained in the future. Not exactly a comforting thought.

Maybe she could eliminate that possibility once the mugger and thief were caught. She'd do anything to help Hal lock them up.

She pushed in the door and smiled at the clanging of Granny's beat-up old cowbell. The woman was a character. Everyone loved her. Even though she did meddle in their lives. They all knew it was done out of an abundance of loving concern for "her" folks, as she called the residents of Loganton.

"'Morning, Steph," the sassy senior chirped as she tied a massive white apron around her thin frame. "You almost beat me here from church. You and the sheriff."

Steph cast a glance in the direction Granny jabbed her chin to see Hal in the last booth on the left side. She smiled and nodded politely, but when she went to take the table closest to the door, he waved her over.

"Please join me," he called.

"A course she's gonna join you, Hal," Granny said, bustling over. "She's no dummy." The diner owner gave Steph a gentle push. "Go on. Don't let the boy sit there waiting on you. Have mercy, girl! It's no wonder y'aren't married yet. Not if you're gonna drag your feet like this anytime a man invites you."

By then, Steph's cheeks felt hotter than Granny's grill. There was no polite way to avoid it, so she walked down the diner's aisle. At the sheriff's booth, she paused.

"I really don't want to impose—"

"You're not imposing. I asked you to join me." His brown

eyes reminded her of a cup of coffee, rich and complex in color and depth, definitely hard to refuse. "Please."

What woman could say no?

"I'm sure you were hoping for a quiet Sunday meal," she said, her cheeks hotter than ever. "The last thing you'd want is to dissect a case."

He leaned back against the red vinyl seat and studied her. "Funny, you don't look like a case, basket or otherwise."

The laugh escaped before she could stop it. "That was awful!"

"Made you laugh, didn't I?"

"Sometimes there's nothing to do but laugh in the face of the ridiculous."

"I'll admit, my pun was pretty bad, but from where I'm sitting, your smile was well worth it."

"You make me sound ever so pleasant."

At his arched brow, she went on. "Sure. You have to stoop to puns of the worst kind to get something other than doom or gloom out of me. But I'm not really like that. Not usually." She took a deep breath. "You'll have to admit, I haven't had the most normal of weeks."

He ran a finger around the edge of his coffee cup, then, without looking up, gave her a nod. "I'll grant you that. It was pretty crazy. Don't remember a time when I've been called to the same crime scene three times in four days."

Although his words were said in a mild voice, the look he finally gave her didn't strike Steph as anything other than piercing, assessing and perceptive.

She stiffened. "What is that supposed to mean?"

With a shrug, he lifted the cup to his lips. Steph shot Granny a plea, wondering when the woman would provide her with at the very least the means with which to occupy her hands and mouth. Not to mention the shot of caffeine that might just help sharpen her thoughts. She hadn't had even a sip yet; her alarm clock hadn't gone off, and she'd run late to church that morning.

"I didn't mean anything by that," he said. "I only stated a fact. I've never been called out to the same location for a series of crimes that close to each other. Even you have to admit that is…odd."

Steph got the impression he'd wanted to say something stronger than a bland "odd," but he'd wisely held back his initial choice. "It's odd, but not if you realize that I'm being targeted because of what I sell in the store. The drug culture isn't exactly known for halfhearted measures."

"True."

Granny finally showed up with the mug of java. Steph wrapped her now-chilled hands around the hot white china. As she drew a deep breath of the rich brew's scent, Granny pulled out the pencil she always wore stuck in the tight silver bun on the top of her head and poised it over her order pad. "What'll you two be having this time? If you can stand a suggestion, I'll tell you my pumpkin spice pancakes are sure good today."

Familiar with Granny's skill in the kitchen, Steph didn't for a moment doubt the woman's claim. She agreed to the pancakes, a glass of fresh-pressed apple juice from a nearby orchard's harvest and a thick slice of Canadian bacon, sizzled to a golden tinge on the hot grill. The sheriff ordered the same.

"Now go on and wipe off those gloomy looks, will ya?" Granny said, a disgusted frown on her wizened face. "What good's gonna come outta you two sitting here and eating my good food if all's you're gonna do is talk crooks and crime the whole time? I don't sell any of them antacids like you do, Steph."

As she hustled toward the kitchen, Hal chuckled. "She's right, you know. It's Sunday, I can't get anything back from the lab until tomorrow and I don't think it'd be wise for you to open up the store, since this is your typical day off. No need to give the perp a reason to…oh, I don't know. Try a do-over?"

"He might have a harder time if he tries again," she said. "I checked out surveillance cameras on the Internet last night, and I ordered some. They'll be here in a day or two."

"Good move."

"And, if he tries to tackle me another time, he'll have two of us to deal with. I just hired Darcy to clean the place for me. She'll come at around six, when I close, and then we'll both leave together."

"You'll kill two birds with one friend. You'll get a clean store, and you'll also get yourself some safety in numbers. Since you didn't have cameras, the buddy system would have been a great help last Wednesday."

She shivered. "That was the last day my life was normal."

He ran his fingers through his hair. "You're right. Nothing's been normal this week."

Although she'd never been confrontational, she'd also never faced a situation like this. The memory of the questions the cops had aimed her way popped back into her thoughts. "Tell me honestly, Sheriff Benson. Do you think I could be so negligent as to forget to lock up a place full of lifesaving— and potentially life-ending—products?"

She continued to stare at Hal until he reluctantly met her gaze. "I don't think you're a careless woman, but anyone can make a mistake. And you'd just had some very stressful, difficult days. Anything could have slipped your mind—"

"I have my answer, then." She shook her head. "Don't try to wiggle out of what you just told me. You did say it. That's enough for me."

"I didn't say anything so horrible. I just acknowledged the possibility of a slipup."

She crossed her arms. "Did you see me *slip up?* Did you watch me rush out of the store without paying attention to what I was doing? You were there, you know. You saw everything I did the night before the break-in. How careless was I?"

It struck her the sheriff wasn't used to being challenged. He looked none too pleased with her questions. But they were fair. He had been with her when she'd closed up.

"I never called you careless."

She went to argue the point, but the way he arched his brow stopped her.

He continued. "What I do think is that you might have missed one small step in your routine because you were— understandably—rattled by the events of the previous couple days. I wasn't passing judgment."

"Did I lock the grate over the pharmacy counter?"

"I seem to remember you doing so."

"Did I lock the door to the pharmacy?"

"I seem to remember you doing that, too, but—"

"There are no buts here, Sheriff. Either I locked up and you saw me do it or you weren't paying attention."

"How can you be so sure you didn't forget?"

Did she dare go ahead and explain how she fought her daily battle with the Beast? Would he understand? Or would he use her disability to condemn her further?

As she weighed her options, Steph studied the man across the table from her. Golden brown hair settled in a slight wave away from his high forehead. Dark brows arched over his warm brown eyes, and crinkles at the corners told her he either squinted into the sun more than he should or else he smiled easily and frequently. She knew which of the two choices she preferred. His generous mouth wore a bracket of lines at the corners, and slight dimples echoed those lines just a bit farther along the plane of cheek beneath angular cheekbones. It looked like the smile theory was the right one in his case.

All in all, Hal Benson was a good-looking man, his face manly and craggy in the right places, gentle and kind in the right places, too.

Steph drew in a calming breath. "Do you know anything about attention deficit disorder?"

"Just that it makes kids antsy and itchy and keeps them from doing well in school."

"That's the stereotype, but there are different ways the condition manifests itself." She pinned him with her gaze. "Do you remember me as antsy and itchy when we were back in school?"

He snorted. "You were the total opposite. You were so quiet and busy in a world all your own that I hardly ever heard you speak—unless it was in whispers with Darcy. You're not trying to tell me you have ADD, are you?"

"That's exactly what I'm telling you. A wonderful counselor who specializes in learning disabilities finally diagnosed me in college. My daydreaming was part of the condition."

"Okay. I'll buy the daydreaming, but you never disrupted class or anything. You weren't busy jumping around or chattering all the time."

"That's because I don't have the H part, the hyperactivity component. I have attention deficit disorder *without* hyperactivity. It's more common in girls than boys."

His eyebrows drew together. "What does this have to do with locking up the pharmacy?"

"Nothing and everything." At his skeptical expression, she went on. "A person with ADD tends to be forgetful, especially if she's the kind with the tendency to daydream. We both know that's me."

"But that would seem to confirm what I suggested."

"*If* I hadn't gone through counseling to develop ways to cope with the condition. I learned to come up with routines I can follow consistently so that I don't run the risk of letting the ADD beat me when it really matters."

"And…?"

"And I have a rigid series of steps I take to close up in the evening. That pattern has become second nature after five years of running the store. It's as much a part of me as breathing and blinking. I didn't forget to lock up that night."

The line of his jaw struck her as a touch hard and set. "It would seem more likely that someone with your condition might miss a step here or there, especially when they're stressed out. Doesn't stress aggravate learning disabilities?"

Granny chose that moment to hustle up, platters filled with the great-smelling brunches in hand. "Hmph! What did I tell ya? You weren't s'posed to be talking shop. Now here I'm bringing you nice food, and y'all are gonna sour it all up by talking about your nasty mess over at the store."

Steph looked up into wise blue eyes. "It looks as though the sheriff has the bigger problem between us, Granny. My problems are the mugger, the vandal and the thief who is still out there with a bunch of missing meds." She glanced at Hal, whose jaw now looked like a chunk of granite. "He's having trouble figuring out who's guilty of what. And that's on top of having to catch those three—or maybe it's just one who's guilty of all three crimes."

The look of irritation Hal shot her almost made Steph regret her comment. Almost. It burned her that someone who'd grown up with her could think her capable of such carelessness when it came to people's lives.

"Don't pay that no never mind," Granny countered. "Hal's a smart boy. He'll get it right. And sooner rather than later, too. Now, I mean it. Eat, and don't you go bringing troubles to one of my tables, either one of you. That's not what I use to season my food, after all."

As she bustled away, Steph heard the diner's owner muttering about their lack of common sense, romance and their failure to find mates. Her cheeks blazed again, and this time, she lacked the courage to even glance at the sheriff. She turned instead to the fragrant food and dug in.

Fortunately, the pumpkin pancakes were as good as Granny had said.

As she ate, something tickled the edges of Steph's memory, something important, something she couldn't quite latch on to but tried with all her powers of concentration, which were, admittedly, less than stellar. Then it hit her.

"That's it!" Her fork clattered against the thick, white ironstone plate. "Of course, I didn't forget to lock up. You even said there was…oh, I can't remember exactly what—maybe wax?—on the lock. The thief made a copy of the key to get in. I told you I didn't leave anything unlocked."

"That was the outside door, Steph," Hal said in a gentle voice. "We're talking about the inner one to the pharmacy. We know how he got into the store. But how did he get past your steel door? We found no wax there."

She sank back into the seat, her appetite gone. "Oh."

"That's where the possibility of skipping a lock comes in."

"But isn't that too great a coincidence? That a thief would break in the one and only night I theoretically—and only theoretically, since I know I didn't forget any of the steps in my routine—missed that most important door?"

That made him uncomfortable. Something else occurred to her.

She narrowed her gaze. "Don't you even think to suggest

I might have had something to do with someone getting into the store and stealing the pseudoephedrine, either. I pulled it off my shelves and stashed it behind the counter the minute a flash alert notified pharmacists to do so. I didn't waste a second. And I'd already started my visits to the schools with my antidrug program. I don't do drugs—in any way."

His shoulders rose and fell with his deep, rough breath. "They got in somehow."

"But not because of me. You watched me lock up, and you agree the too-coincidental possibility is a big stretch."

"I followed you as you locked up, but I wasn't exactly focused on your every last action."

Steph leaned forward, stared straight at him. "Then what were you watching, if not my closing procedures?"

"Well, well, well!"

Ed Townsend's voice had the same effect on Steph as nails on a chalkboard.

"Isn't this interesting," the lawyer said. "Our sheriff and the pharmacist all cozy over breakfast. And now we learn he was there with her when she blew it locking up the *drugs*. Looks like a clear case of dereliction of duty…or malfeasance…collusion, or maybe even law enforcement malpractice."

The delight on his too-thin face made Steph itch to rub it off, but the thought of touching the miserable man kept her a safe distance away. She turned to Hal. The muscles in his cheeks and jaw worked as he fought to keep some kind of response from spurting out—or at least, that's how it looked to her. Finally, when his fists sat on the table and his shoulders rode back, his head rising tall and his eyes narrowed, he stood to face his nemesis.

"There's no such thing as law enforcement malpractice,

and you know it, Ed. Go chase an ambulance somewhere. I have the county's business to see to."

"Not for long," Ed crowed. "Not for long, *Sheriff* Benson."

Hal stalked away from the booth.

Steph watched him leave.

At the cash register, he yanked out his wallet, dragged out a couple of bills, dropped them on the counter and then continued on his way out.

"A guilty conscience does things to a man's manners," Ed added after the door swished closed.

Steph rolled her eyes, grabbed her purse and stood. "It's too bad I don't carry a mirror in my purse, then. It would do a good job of showing you the guilty party in the matter of manners."

As she neared the register, Granny winked and started to clap. "You go, Steph, girl. Way to tell Ed what's what."

She delved into her bag for her wallet, but Granny shook her head. "With what that boy dropped, you and he both have at least three meals each in credit here. Go ahead."

On her way down the diner's front steps, Steph heard Granny lay into Ed. "I've told you a million times if I ever told you once, Ed Townsend. You got yourself a mouth like a mad rattler's poison. I thank the good Lord your sweet mama isn't with us any longer to hear what you just said, her being such a lovely Christian woman and all. This ain't no way to win an election…"

Granny was right. Steph smiled. The owner of the diner wasn't someone you wanted riled up against you. She told it plain as plain and tart as sour cherries. By the time the older woman was done with him, Ed would be begging to ask Hal's forgiveness.

At least, he would be if he had a conscience.

Or an ounce of character.

* * *

On his way home, Hal called himself all kinds of fool. How could he have let Ed get the better of him like that?

He knew he shouldn't let the pompous lawyer's taunts and barbs crawl under his skin, no matter how stinging or nasty they might be. All Ed wanted was to catch Hal in the worst possible light, then exploit it to the benefit of his so-called campaign. The only thing the lawyer cared about was winning the election. And for what? For the love of serving others?

Nope. Ed was only after the status the title would give him. And a hand up the political ladder.

Hal didn't think Ed cared one whit about the county's citizens, much less their protection or their well-being.

As a matter of fact, Ed hadn't taken one single case to court yet. So far, all he'd done since coming home clutching a still damp-inked diploma and passing the state bar exam was to talk his relatives into letting him write wills for them. Nothing too challenging. And while Hal hadn't heard whether he was competent in that endeavor or not, he figured the wills at least must be legal.

But dealing with the day-to-day details of keeping track of crime and safety in the county? Hal knew with heart-deep certainty that Ed didn't have what it took to tackle getting his hands dirty with something like dog catching, much less fighting for anything of greater consequence.

Now Ethan Rodgers…he was a different story. Unease settled in Hal's stomach when he thought of the former DEA agent. Was Hal out of his league with this investigation into the missing pseudoephedrine? Was the former big-city DEA agent better equipped to handle a case like this? What about all the other aspects of county law enforcement? Would someone whose specialty was drug crime handle DUIs and traffic issues on the freeway or home evictions equally well?

Hal was the sheriff. He excelled at his job. Maybe Ethan would be a good resource during this investigation, but the Chicago native didn't know the county. He'd lived in Loganton no more than two years—if that. Hal, on the other hand, knew his jurisdiction like his well-shaven chin. He'd grown up locally, and he'd known the people he dealt with on a daily basis his whole life. It would take Ethan Rodgers years to get up to speed with the multitude of local nuances and details.

If worse came to worse, Hal figured the former DEA agent had to be a competent investigator. Ed seemed to lack even the slightest aptitude for…well, for just about anything. Anything other than writing wills.

And driving Hal crazy.

SIX

Driving home, Steph couldn't escape the memory of Hal's distress at Ed Townsend's obnoxious comments. Yes, the sheriff had given her a touch of heartburn, what with his questions and suspicion.

Oh, all right. One of the things that burned the most was Hal calling her professionalism into question. Steph treasured her career. She loved serving others and did everything possible to increase her knowledge and competence. Because of that, she could understand Hal's frustration in the face of Ed's insinuations.

Two blocks down the road, she noticed a blue car driving too close to the back of hers. She slowed to let the midsize sedan go by, but it slowed down, too, and stayed put in her rearview mirror. When she reached the intersection of Main Street and Walnut, while she waited for the red light to turn green, she tried to see who was behind the wheel, squinting and leaning from side to side. Unfortunately, the sun's glare on the blue car's windshield made it impossible to make out more than the vague figure of a driver.

When the light changed, she headed out toward her carriage house on the outskirts of town. But as soon as she left the more congested center of Loganton, the blue car again began to ride her rear bumper. This time, she pulled over to the shoulder, lowered her window and waved the car on by.

That's what it did…until it came nose to nose with her. Then the passenger-side window lowered, and next thing she knew, a solid gray blur flew at her. A second before it struck, she identified the missile, a rock. Her windshield shattered into a million shards.

A scream tore from her throat. She slammed on the brakes and crossed her arms over her face to protect herself. The steering wheel spun, veering her off the road.

The car jerked to a halt.

Her engine hummed.

No blue car.

Steph sat for a second…five, heart pounding, fear churning in her gut, tears rolling down her cheeks. A sob shot up and burst from her lips.

Who would do such a thing?

Her hands shook, and it was all Steph could do to turn the key in the ignition. She knew who could do such a thing. It was obvious.

The mugger could do it.

So could the pseudoephedrine thief.

With every ounce of determination she could call up, Steph forced herself to control the shaking enough to dig through her purse for her cell phone. She flipped it open then dialed 911, her fingers weak, random shudders wracking her.

When the dispatcher answered, Steph found she couldn't eke out a word. The woman said "Hello" a number of times, each greeting angrier than the last.

"Prank calls are prosecutable, you know," she added, her voice terse. "And we will track you down."

The last thing Steph needed was another reason for the

authorities to want to lock her up. "S-sorry," she managed, her voice barely more than a whisper. "I need help. My car…off the road…"

After she croaked out her name and directions, Steph closed the phone and let her head drop against the headrest. The shaking hadn't stopped, but it had eased enough that she thought she'd be able to stand once the police officers arrived.

She groaned. Police.

Again.

The thought of another grilling by the authorities was almost more than she could bear. This one, though, might have a silver lining. They couldn't possibly think she'd thrown a rock at her own windshield while driving. It was physically impossible.

True, they might try to say she'd driven the car off the road, gotten out and only then busted the glass. She rubbed her forearm. If they tried that theory on for size, they'd have to try awfully hard to explain how she'd done that and still wound up with the small cuts where bits of broken glass had struck her arms.

Maybe now Hal Benson would believe she hadn't had anything to do with the missing drugs.

From the direction of town, she heard a siren approach, its piercing sound growing louder as it came. Her initial relief, though, soon vanished. Her body refused to obey her brain's commands. Her fingers fumbled with the door handle. After four futile attempts, she finally succeeded in opening her door.

Then she had to really focus, to redouble her efforts. Her legs felt like jelly, and her head swam. Her stomach lurched each time she moved. Adrenaline did a number on a body, but knowing what was causing her struggles didn't help her overcome them.

Little by little, Steph called on her willpower to impose control over her body. By the time the cruiser pulled up behind her car, she was standing, propped up against the rear door, ready, she hoped, to deal with the cops' questions.

When Hal unfolded his long body from behind the wheel of his official vehicle, she let out a good, strong groan. That she managed to make the sound was a victory of sorts, but her situation couldn't have been worse.

Well, it could… She shuddered as her fertile imagination conjured images of what else the windshield-breaker might have done.

"I had my radio on," Hal said, walking to her side. "I heard the dispatcher, so I took a detour on my way home. What happened?"

In spite of her groan and unsure of her voice, she pointed to the shattered glass.

Hal's eyebrows rose. He stepped around her, leaned over the fender to get a better look at the damage and then offered a noncommittal "Hmm…"

"What…what does that mean?" she asked.

"It means there's a nice big rock sitting on top of one wiper blade. We can safely assume that's what trashed your windshield."

She shrugged. "One moment, I'm moving over to let the blue car go by, and the next…" She waved toward the front of the car. "It burst and some of the glass hit me…you get the picture."

He tightened his jaw. "Too well."

The Loganton PD's patrol car pulled up, and Maggie Lowe and Wayne Donnelly got out. From the look Officer Donnelly sent Steph, she knew she would have an even harder time convincing them she hadn't had anything to do with the theft and break-in at her store or with this latest disaster than she'd had with Hal. She wasn't sure she blamed them, either. Too many incidents piled up, one after the other, didn't conjure up visions of coincidence.

She crossed her arms to keep the still-lingering shivers to a minimum and winced. A glance showed her the pinprick cuts, some with tiny slivers of glass still in them. At least she'd blocked them with her arms. She hated to think what would have happened if they'd struck her face…her eyes.

"Are you okay?" Officer Lowe asked.

Steph shrugged. "A couple of scratches from the broken glass is all."

The police officer glanced at the shattered windshield. "You're lucky you live in the age of tempered glass. I'd hate to think what might have happened if your car hadn't had it."

Another shudder ran through Steph. "Then let's not."

She waved the cops toward the car as she stepped away. Fortunately, her legs had decided to work again, and she didn't embarrass herself by tripping. While the three law enforcement officers went about their work, she watched, taking note of what they checked, what they measured, what they gathered with their gloved hands and stored in clear plastic zippered bags. The rock seemed to Steph the most important piece of evidence.

After about twenty minutes of meticulous work on their part, Maggie approached, one of those bags in her hand. "Take a look at this. Any ideas?"

Steph stared through the clear plastic. "Stay away from the cops" was written in black marker on the flat side of the rock. A shudder ran through her, and she shook her head.

Officer Donnelly separated himself from the others and approached Steph. "Someone doesn't want you to report the mishaps you've been having. Who'd you make so mad they'd do this to you?"

Steph squared her shoulders. There it was, that hint of suspicion. And even though she couldn't blame Officer Donnelly, seeing how things had come about, she still didn't like it.

"I don't go around antagonizing my customers—bad for business, you know—or anyone else, for that matter. Don't let the negative side of your work spill over and color how you see me." A moment later, she added, "Please."

The cop's ears reddened, and from the front of her car, Steph heard a poorly muffled chuckle. When she looked to see which of the two remaining officers she'd amused, they both appeared consumed by their investigative efforts.

Officer Donnelly took out the ever-present notebook and pen and took a deep breath. Before he could ask, she started.

"I'd just finished having breakfast at Granny's with Sheriff Benson—" shaggy brows shot up; the pen danced over the page "—and was on my way home…"

When Steph came to the end of her tale, the cop had only filled one and a half pages of his pad, far fewer scribbles than he'd racked up the previous times they'd come face-to-face.

His frown told her he was well aware of the lack. "And that's it?"

"What else do you want me to say? I drove out, stopped at a light, tried to see who was following too close, didn't make out anything, kept going, waved them by, then had my windshield smashed with a rock."

Officer Donnelly tipped up his hat, looked her in the eye. "Where'd that other car go? Blue, did you say it was?"

She swallowed hard and met his gaze. "I wouldn't really expect him to hang around." She paused for a beat. "Not unless you think he might have wanted to wait and see if I made it and then come finish me off."

He glanced up from his notes. "Then all I have to go on is you telling me about some other car, your locked door at the pharmacy counter and some mugger out back of your store."

"I called you because it was serious. And trust me, I didn't give myself scraped knees in the alley or cuts from the splintered windshield. Your doubt is not something I enjoy, nor is the reality of stolen items for which my business paid and will never recoup the costs. I'm not drowning in dollars."

"Lay off Miss Scott, Wayne," Officer Lowe said. "Mr. Cooper saw someone beating up on her out in the alley. Besides, she couldn't have thrown the rock at her windshield and cut herself at the same time."

Steph sent the petite policewoman a grateful smile. But the woman's serious expression sent the smile fleeing. Great. What now?

"Is there someone you can call for a ride home?" Officer Lowe asked. "We have to impound the car. It's evidence now."

She couldn't call Mom or Dad. They'd go ballistic and insist she move back in with them. Oh, she knew she had to tell them what was happening, but this wasn't the way for them to find out. The best thing to do would be to hit Darcy up for a ride. She made the call.

As she waited for her friend to show up, Steph gnawed on her bottom lip. She watched the cops work the scene. After a few minutes, Hal called for a tow truck while Officers Donnelly and Lowe studied the tire tracks her car left when it went off the road.

"This is escalating. If you'd lost control of the car, you could have been killed," Hal said.

Finally, when Darcy pulled up in her rolling wreck, Steph

checked with Hal to see if they were going to say they needed her purse or if she could take it with her. Once he gave her a brief nod of approval, she climbed in.

"You look awful," Darcy said, concern on her face. "And your car! What are you going to do for wheels now?"

Steph shrugged. "I'll have to shell out for a rental. I need to get out to the elementary school on Tuesday morning, and since I canceled yesterday's session at The Pines, I can't skip out on the seniors next Saturday. They've come to count on me to help them with minor medical questions."

"Ouch! A rental will suck your wallet dry."

"Let's talk about that wallet once I get my car back, okay? We'll see then how dry the rental sucked it. Come on. I want to get to the hospital. I'm tired of playing pincushion to these bits of glass. They hurt, and I don't want to make matters worse by trying to take them out myself."

In her usual zippy fashion, Darcy sped away, spitting gravel from her tires at the three cops. Steph cringed. Those were *cops* out there. "What are you thinking? Do you want them to lock me up for sure?"

Darcy glanced at Steph, blew a bubble and grinned. "They're busy. Besides, this thing only goes from zero to…oh, about eight miles an hour in fifteen seconds flat! They can't even nail me for speeding."

As old as Darcy's car was, Steph knew her friend had a point. But no matter how she tried, she knew Officers Donnelly and Lowe, and even Sheriff Benson, weren't fully sure they believed anything Steph told them. She turned partway around. As Darcy's car chugged away toward the hospital, the three cops stared at them going up the road.

Donnelly looked suspicious.

Lowe, doubtful.

Hal smiled.

That smile gave Steph's drooping optimism a boost. Things weren't so bad after all. She was innocent—that was a fact. The sheriff had a sense of humor.

Hope was a beautiful light, even in the midst of trouble.

"What have you found so far?" Hal asked, his gaze on the disappearing rattletrap Darcy still drove after all these years.

Wayne spat. "Other than the rock warning her, nothing. A great big load of nothing."

Hal crossed his arms. "Can you be a little more specific here? What exactly do you mean by nothing?"

The older cop took a step forward, but Maggie placed a hand on his arm. "Let me, okay?" She turned to Hal. "What Wayne *so* eloquently meant is that we have found absolutely no evidence of another person going into that pharmacy. If it weren't for Mr. Cooper, who did see someone attack Steph…well, I'd have to say she was involved somehow."

Hal's stomach tightened. That wasn't what he'd wanted to hear, even though he'd come close to saying something similar to Steph himself. "Why?"

"Why?" Maggie asked. "Why what?"

"Why would you think Steph was involved?"

"Come on, Hal," Wayne said. "Don't tell me you haven't heard how many of these pharmacists get themselves hooked on the stuff they're supposed to be selling. It's like the kid in the candy store thing."

Reason told Hal that Wayne was right. Something inside him, some leftover part of the teen who'd fallen for Steph Scott, recoiled. "I don't know how the thief got into the pharmacy. But would Steph go to all that trouble just to steal the drugs she has at her fingertips? I don't think so. This brings too much attention to the missing stuff."

Maggie nudged a pebble with the toe of her regulation oxford. "She might if she was trying to draw the attention away from her."

"Do *you* think she's a junkie?" he asked, his voice challenging, determined. They'd notice his insistence, his dwindling professional detachment, but he didn't care. Much.

Maggie shrugged. "I don't know Steph well enough to say. It would take someone who's known her a long time to be able to say whether they've seen a change in her or not."

He sucked in a harsh breath.

"Someone like you," Wayne said, his gaze on Hal's face. "You went to school with Steph Scott, didn't you, Sheriff?"

His own past had just trapped him. "Yes, of course I did. I grew up here. Even so, I don't know that I would be able to tell whether Steph has changed or not."

"Why would that be?" Maggie asked.

How did he explain Steph's ADD without pointing the finger of suspicion at her again? "Because she was very quiet in school. She only hung out with Darcy Thomas, and they never got in trouble."

"So trouble would be out of character." Maggie didn't ask; she stated.

"I believe so."

Pugnacious as ever, Wayne crossed his arms, pen in one hand, notepad in the other. "But you can't know what happened while she was off to Chapel Hill for school all those years." The older man had always reminded Hal of a bulldog, a quality he usually admired and respected, since it brought about excellent results. Now…? Well, he didn't like it so much when the man applied it to Steph's case.

He shrugged. "You never can tell about anyone, Wayne. Not for sure. But I can reasonably say I doubt Steph's the kind of person who would resort to drugs."

"How about money?" Maggie asked.

"Does it look to you like she's living rich?"

Wayne stuffed the notepad in his pocket. "No, but what if she's really having trouble rubbing two nickels together? Drugs are easy money—until you get caught."

Yeah, but… "Is that why she's been slashing merchandise boxes? Why she 'stole' a pile of meds she could have sold? For the money she won't make back now? Is that why she would make it so she has to call out a locksmith to replace all her locks? Plus the surveillance equipment. I'll bet all that set her back some bucks."

His argument got him nowhere. He tried again. "Do you think she went so far as to scribble on a rock and break the windshield herself? If that's what you think, then you're going to have to explain to me how she got glass on her arms."

"Well, well, well, Maggie my girl." Wayne shook his head. "I guess maybe Ed Townsend does have a point. He says Sheriff Benson can't keep his head on this job 'cause he's been sweet on Steph Scott since the time they were kids."

Easy, Hal. Go easy.

He forced out a pretty good chuckle. "Are you telling me you're falling for Ed's wacky so-called campaign tactics?" When Wayne's cheeks reddened, Hal went on. "Why, Officer Donnelly? I would have expected better from you. You're an experienced investigator. You don't need to listen to a wannabe who's only after my job so he can play cops and robbers. And not too well at that, I'm afraid."

The tow truck pulled up just then. Fortunately for Hal.

"Maybe I shouldn't," Wayne said, sauntering toward the

vehicle. "But she might have had a partner, someone who pitched the rock at her car. So forgive me, Sheriff, but I won't take your word either." Three steps later, he tossed over his shoulder his parting shot. "Or hers."

A silent Maggie followed her partner.

Hal watched.

Why? Why had he defended Steph so passionately? He'd followed a similar tack to Wayne's at the diner not that much earlier. Had he really become that biased because of his ever-deepening, complicated feelings for Steph? Had he lost all objectivity just because of Wayne's and Maggie's suspicions?

If that was the case, then he might do Steph more harm than good. He stayed by her car, mulling over his thoughts, and let Wayne and Maggie deal with the tow truck driver. Not another word was exchanged until their blunt goodbyes rang out.

Behind the wheel once again, headed toward his house and Pepper, Hal made himself face the truth. The boy who'd pined for Steph Scott from afar didn't *want* to think she could be involved in anything illegal. By the same token, his years of law enforcement service forced him to consider the possibility.

If he was ever going to protect her, he would not only have to consider that possibility but he'd also have to prove or disprove it. That was the only way he'd ever be sure of her innocence.

As irrational as it might be, he didn't *think* she was implicated, he was actually *afraid* she might be implicated. And he was making a big deal of the difference.

Help me, Lord. I'm afraid I'm in over my head.

Tuesday morning found Hal on the road to Loganton Elementary School. He needed to see for himself how Steph handled her drug awareness program. He felt anyone even remotely involved in the drug trade would be unable to come across as sincere in an effort to denounce it.

He'd spent hours praying and even more hours looking into Steph's past. There'd been nothing to find—or at least, that was how he saw it. A call to Chapel Hill police had produced nothing. The university also could only quote glowing reports from her professors. And the citizens of Loganton, to a one, vouched for Steph's character.

As did Pastor Art Reams, a man Hal trusted.

So far, so good.

Now, he wanted to watch her in action. He hoped seeing would be believing.

He pulled into the parking lot, ran up to the door, buzzed for security to let him into the building and then followed the secretary to the classroom where Steph was doing her thing, unable to give the woman the attention she deserved as she sang the pretty pharmacist's praises.

The last thing Hal expected was exactly what he found. Around the otherwise typical fourth-grade classroom, Steph had hung a number of posters, extraordinarily graphic pictures he would have hesitated to show such young kids had he been the one giving the presentation. One black and white depicted the remains of an abandoned meth lab, the containers of antifreeze, paint thinner, miles of tubing and beakers, some intact, most broken, offering stark evidence of an explosion.

But the photo that hit Hal the hardest was one of a teen, her youthful beauty stolen by the ravages wrought by her abuse of methamphetamine. The girl was emaciated, her hair strawlike and disheveled, her eyes sunken and ringed in smudgy purple and black shadows. Her lips were parted, and one could clearly make out her ruined teeth, while her complexion was pocked with the sores common to meth users. It didn't take long for meth to do its worst.

"…My heart breaks every time I see this photo," Steph said, anguish in her voice, sadness on her face. "She's only seventeen, and has hurt her body in ways that can't fully be reversed."

As she spoke, she smoothed gentle fingers over the paper image of the girl's features, compassionate, tender, worried and caring. Even though he stood on the other side of the doorway to the classroom, Hal could still see the glimmer of tears in Steph's gray eyes. Then, as if she'd just realized what she'd done, she drew back her hand, brought it to her waist and covered it with the other.

"The reason I'm here," she said, "is because I don't want any of you to end up like her." She swept the students with her gaze, an expression of infinite tenderness on her face. "Not you…or you…or you, either. I want you well and strong and smart. Alive."

The room fell silent. Time stopped.

Powerful.

Then Hal heard a sigh. A sniff. The kids were riveted to Steph's words.

He didn't blame them. He was, too.

"Lord?" he whispered.

"Do any of you have any questions for me?" Steph asked.

He had dozens. But one, maybe the most important one, she'd already answered. Without any proof, Hal knew she'd had nothing to do with the theft at her pharmacy. Lacking that proof, however, presented him with a major problem.

"Father, help me help her."

True, he had no answers. Yet.

He did, however, have faith.

SEVEN

Every year, during the second week of October, Loganton celebrated its Fall Fest. During those fun days, the kids at school were treated to special activities and treats, shop owners held to special hours and on Saturday afternoon, the local PD closed Main Street so that booths could line the sidewalks. Not only did local businesses offer discounted merchandise and special bargains, but crafters also sold gifts of all sorts for the upcoming holidays. Anything to boost the town's economic outlook was welcome by all.

Steph had always loved the excitement of the Fall Fest. Apple cider, popcorn balls and sloppy joe sandwiches had a permanent home in her memories of the yearly event. Usually she couldn't wait for October to roll around. This year? Hmm....

The events at her store and on the road to her home two Sundays ago had stolen Steph's sense of excited anticipation. She hadn't known how she was going to handle keeping her store open while she manned the booth outside until Darcy offered to help. She'd taken her friend up on the offer, but Steph still wasn't sure how things would turn out. The last thing she wanted was another episode of vandalism, much less to involve Darcy or Jimmy in the whole sorry mess.

She refused to consider the possibility of another break-in.

On Saturday morning, by the time Steph got to the store, Darcy was waiting outside.

"Hey, there, you early worm, you!" Steph called out. "I'm so glad you were able to give me a hand. There's no way Jimmy and I can take care of everything by ourselves."

"What are friends for?" Darcy rubbed her hands together. "Brrr! Can you believe how cold it got last night? I hope that doesn't cut down on the number of people who'll come out for the festival."

"Don't even think that. I can't afford to lose the business."

"Steph!" Granny called, hurrying toward them as the friends headed into the store. "Wait up a minute, girl. I'm too old for all this running!"

Steph turned around. She grinned. Now *there* was an unusual sight. Five-foot-nothing Granny charged up the street, swathed in her voluminous apron, the eraser end of her pencil bouncing out of the bun on her head, as she dragged six-foot-three Hal Benson in her wake. In the sassy senior's other age-spotted hand she clutched a fat bundle of paper. When she reached the drugstore, she waved the sheets at Steph.

"Here you go," Granny said, huffing and puffing from the exertion. "We need your help. There's no way this county can stand a minute of that dunderheaded Ed Townsend playacting sheriff. You can hand out flyers for Hal's campaign to everyone who buys foot fungus powder or bad breath gargle."

It took more effort than she would have imagined to smother a laugh. Steph glanced at Hal. "Do you expect so much trouble that you'll be too busy to campaign?"

He shrugged, a twinkle in his eye. "I'm on the job, but Granny is, too. I surrendered to her greater wisdom and longer phone number list. She's my new campaign manager."

At Steph's side, Darcy made a choked sound. Steph refused

to look, but by the same measure, she also refused to meet Hal's gaze again. She'd never do anything to hurt the diner owner's feelings, and Granny Annie's expression displayed a surplus of earnest intent. She clearly meant well. Even if she was funny.

Besides, Steph agreed with the woman. "You're right," she said, taking the bundle of paper. "We can't let Ed take the county apart bit by incompetent bit. Every bottle of aspirin or tube of deodorant will have a flyer tucked in the bag for my customers' benefit—and Hal's."

"Ahem!" Darcy offered. "And may the best man win."

Steph laughed, as did the others, and then Granny spun away. "Gotta run, gotta run! Who knows how many orders Karla's written up for me while I've been busy managing the sheriff's election," she said, waving goodbye. "Got me some hungry people and plenty of cooking to do back at the diner. See? A woman's work is never done, ya know."

To Steph's surprise, Hal followed her and Darcy into the store. She handed her friend the steel cash box she used for sidewalk sales and sent her out to man the booth. Jimmy dashed in, running late, then went straight to the back room for his broom. His first job was always to sweep the sidewalk out front so customers found Scott's clean and welcoming.

And then it was just the two of them, in the store, facing each other, all alone. Steph had no idea how to handle Hal's presence. She'd never been suspected of any wrongdoing. How was she supposed to act? Should she ignore him?

No. That might make him think she had something to hide.

Well, then, what should she say to him? She'd never been the kind to chatter aimlessly. A slanted glance at the sheriff gave her no guidance. His face remained unreadable, his vague smile neutral, his eyes hidden behind reflective sunglasses.

Oh, brother. She couldn't just stand there feeling awkward.

"Was there something you wanted?" she said when she couldn't stand the silence any longer. "Can I help you find what you're looking for?"

His cheeks colored. "I…um…followed Granny in her 'distribution' mission, since I'm the actual candidate. I didn't think I could in good conscience duck out on her. You know—all those hands to shake. But when I saw you, I…ah…well, I had to confess."

Steph's brows rose. "What to?"

"I spied on you—"

She gasped.

He winced. "That came out all wrong. It's not as bad as it sounds. Really. What I did was watch you teach your drug awareness class at the elementary school."

Anger bubbled up. "Were you afraid I was going to give the kids drugs instead of information?"

He tightened his jaw. "No. I just wanted to see how you approached them, how you related to the kids."

So you could shut me down if I even came close to crossing the line, right?

The repulsive thought sent a chill through her. Steph crossed her arms but didn't know if she was doing it to comfort herself or for protection against Hal's suspicion. "And did I pass muster?"

Hal took off his hat and ran a hand through his brown hair. "This isn't going the way I meant it. I really came to tell you how terrific you were. I was blown away by how much you care for those kids. All I meant was to compliment you on a job very well done."

Steph blinked. Had he said what she thought he'd said? Was the suspicious sheriff saying something good about her? Instead of questioning her motives?

What did she say next?

"Thanks." The warmth of the sheriff's smile touched something deep inside her. Ever since she'd found the second vandalized item, she'd felt alone. She hadn't wanted to involve anyone in her problems, so she hadn't said a word to Darcy, never mind Mom or Dad. But now, Hal was looking at her with something very much like respect. And if she were to believe his words, he really had found something to admire in her. Maybe that appreciation would help temper his suspicion.

But she didn't have the courage to voice the possibility.

If anything, his compliment made her feel more awkward than before. "Ah…well, I do have to open up. I'm sure I'll have customers coming in any minute now."

Hal nodded, turned and walked toward the door. He paused, looked up at the ceiling, over the door, at all four corners, then faced her again. "How about those security cameras you were going to put in?"

Steph pointed. "Take a look at that corner and then over there."

"Good. You needed the added security."

If not the evidence to prove she wasn't the one at fault.

"That's why I did as you suggested."

The awkwardness returned.

Hal tapped the brim of his regulation hat. "I'll be seeing you."

To Steph's surprise, instead of the relief she'd expected to feel once he left, she felt vulnerable and alone again when the door closed behind him.

"Get a hold of yourself, woman!" This was no time to go all sappy because a guy said something nice about her. Yes, the sheriff was an extremely good-looking man. And she knew he was a decent, caring person as well. Even intelligent and devoted to those he was called to serve. An all-around great guy.

But he *was* the sheriff.

Had they met again as adults under different circumstances, she would have liked to get to know him better, maybe even let his appeal lead her into the attraction she fought every time they came face-to-face. As it was, she had too much to lose if the thief got away with…well, with whatever he was up to. With advancing his interests in the drug trade.

And the sheriff *had* been suspicious of her.

Well, he was just going to have to ditch that suspicion, wasn't he? She hadn't done anything wrong or illegal. And she was going to have to find some way to help him do that ditching. Her determination to do so was one of the reasons she'd agreed to let Darcy pitch in and help her outside that day. With three of them on-site, Steph felt fairly certain the thief wouldn't try anything. She hoped to get through the week without another episode.

When she unlocked the pharmacy, a wave of relief hit her. It felt excessive, but when she found everything the way she'd left it the night before, she hoped she'd turned a corner. Ever since the day she'd come in only to find her worst fears had come true, she'd spent hours praying that her added precautions would succeed. Even the antifreeze and paint thinner cans were where she'd left them, out of sight, behind the counter.

She'd decided to take all potential ingredients for that witches' brew off the shelves. She still struggled to understand how anyone could look at those vile chemicals and think of concocting something to put into a human body.

Steph had brought the items behind the counter, even though that kind of control did make more work for her. If anyone wanted to strip paint or keep their radiator running, they would have to come ask her for the products in person.

She'd even started keeping a list of anyone who bought the potential components of the drug. She would do whatever it took to protect her career. She wasn't going to get careless after all those years and all the effort it took to get to where she was.

That was when Chad Adams marched up to the counter, knocked on the window and waved his bag of red licorice. "Gotta get my fix," he said, a crooked grin on his freckled face. "Even if I didn't come in 'cause of work."

Steph rang him up, and he left, a rope of floppy red candy drooping from the corner of his mouth. She wondered if he was trying to quit smoking. She knew many who used gum to keep their mouths busy during those early days, but Chad was the only person she'd known to down so much red licorice.

She didn't have a lot of time to wonder about Chad and his possible habits, though. A stream of seniors from The Pines trooped in, capturing all her attention.

"Hey there, sunshine!" Mason Cutler called out. "D'you have my brilliantine ready for me?"

Steph glanced at the senior citizen's almost hairless head. Why he would want the infamous "greasy kid stuff" of old, she'd never know. "The special orders came in yesterday afternoon, Mr. Cutler. I bagged it up for you, and it's ready to go."

The rest of the day followed in the same vein. As the time flew by, Steph's spirits rose. Some might not think of filling prescriptions for various ailments as a particularly exciting way to earn a living, but she had always felt led to serve her Lord by caring for His children's health.

And today, she was caring for about double the usual number. The flood of folks remained steady and heavy, so much so that by eleven thirty, Darcy stuck her head in the door.

"Could you turn off your laser gizmo on the door?" she

asked, pointing to Steph's very basic alarm system. "It's been buzzing nonstop all morning, and I'm starting to get one fierce headache from all the noise."

Steph laughed. "You know, it's been driving me nuts, too. We don't need it today. There's three of us here and too many people for anyone to try anything funny."

After she disabled the alarm, she found herself a bit more relaxed. Amazing how something as minor as a buzzer could set your nerves on edge. Well, she supposed it wasn't the buzzer that had actually set her nerves on edge; the vandalism, the break-in and the rock on the windshield had done that. But she sure didn't need something zapping her to constant alertness on such a busy day, especially since she had the cameras now.

Mr. Cooper strolled up to the counter. "How've you been since that dreadful night in the alley, Steph?"

She shrugged. "Doing my best. My nerves took the worst hit that night. A scrape on my knees is no big deal."

"Glad to hear. I'm just sorry I couldn't catch the guy."

Me, too. But she didn't add to the man's regrets.

He went on. "I was wondering if that new back support you ordered for me has come in yet."

"The supplier shipped it last Wednesday. I expect it in next Tuesday afternoon's delivery. How about I call you as soon as it comes in?"

"Sounds good." He plunked a box of cotton swabs, a bag of cough lozenges and a thousand-tablet bucket of ibuprofen on the counter.

Steph tapped the pain reliever. "Are you having problems? Arthritis or maybe an injury?"

"Nah. Just stress headaches but a whole bunch of them. Work, and Chad's got himself some problems with another of his crazy schemes. You know how Minnie is. She thinks she's got to go and try to bail out her baby brother every time. And those bills just keep on piling up." He shrugged. "You know. The usual."

Although he'd been pretty reliable since he'd taken the job with Pharmaceutical Suppliers, Chad Adams had a monopoly on the local paper's headlines, and his appearance there was never for a worthwhile reason. From real estate investments in the Mississippi Delta, where even Venice, Italy-style construction wouldn't have helped, to inventions of the left-handed potato peeler sort, Chad had tried them all—and failed—taking his investors' funds down with him.

"I'm sorry to hear of Chad's troubles. I thought he'd settled down."

The postmaster snorted. "Making trouble's what he's settled down to. Like always, he's determined to get something for nothing. I've told him more times than I like to count that while it might not be fun, work, and lots of it, is the only way to make a dime on this earth."

As Mr. Cooper trudged off, Steph welcomed her next customer, this one all smiles. Seventeen-year-old Suzie Cramer was a serious asthmatic as well as a top athlete. Steph had set up a system where she alerted the teen when it was close to the time to order a new rescue inhaler. She didn't want the girl to ever run out of her medication.

"You're getting better at this ordering thing every time," she said, bagging the device.

Suzie tossed her silvery blond mane. "The last one still feels pretty full, but it did sink halfway down in the glass of water when I tested it."

"Good job! That's a good sign you're going to want to

keep a backup on hand. Especially now that basketball season's started."

The high-school girls' team star shot an imaginary basket. "You know it."

More customers followed. The register belted out its song of income, note after satisfying note. Steph hoped it meant she'd be able to make up for the lost revenue from the time the PD shut her down to investigate the break-in.

"Aw, Miss Steph," Jimmy called out at around two fifteen, disgust in his voice. "You gotta come take a look at this."

Unease pooled in Steph's stomach. Praying, she locked the pharmacy door—something she'd never done before the break-in, not just to walk through the store—and hurried to find Jimmy.

Three quarters of the way down the pet supply aisle, she found more than just her part-time store clerk. Knowing how many in town loved their pets, Steph offered numerous brands of cat and dog food, grooming products, treats of all kinds, birdseed, hamster and guinea pig kibble, leashes, collars and even sweaters for cats and dogs. She also kept bags and boxes of kitty litter in stock. One of those boxes held Jimmy's attention.

"What's wrong…?" She let her question dangle. It was only too obvious. Clay pellets from the box had poured down the edge of the shelf and onto the floor, where they pooled in a large pyramid-shaped pile. While she knew better, she tried to discount its significance.

"Oh, probably a poorly glued box," she said, her voice tight.

"Nope," Jimmy countered. "That's what I thought when I first saw the box out of place. But then I took a closer look at this other side. That's when the kitty litter popped out all over the floor."

Steph dropped to one knee. "Oh, great."

A rectangle, about two inches by three, had been sliced out of the side of the box, close to the back corner. The edges were neat, clean and anyone could see a sharp knife had been used. The missing piece of cardboard peeked from under the edge of the mess on the floor, where the weight of the clay chunks had pushed it on their way out. No doubt about it. This was no accident.

But what did a sliced box of kitty litter really mean?

She sighed. "I guess I should call the police. Let them decide if this is important enough to check out or not—they keep telling me I don't have to make that call myself. I only know it's part of a pattern that's driving me nuts."

Maggie Lowe answered her call. "Let me come out and take a look. Nothing official, just to see if there's anything that might help us find this guy."

As she waited, Steph gave in to an inner impulse. She called Hal.

Then, as she waited, she went to retrieve the film from the surveillance cameras. Maggie—and Hal—would want it. But when she got to the first one, a chill ran through her. She ran to the opposite end of the store, and there she found the same thing. The thin wire to the cameras had been cut.

Someone had disabled the cameras. On purpose. And because they only scanned in a straight line instead of up and down there was no way to see who'd done it.

There could be no doubt now. The ruined box of kitty litter wasn't the work of a run-of-the-mill vandal. This was too deliberate. At least there was no twenty-dollar bill this time.

But that didn't tell her why. Or who had done it.

Wrapping her arms around her middle, Steph thought back to the mugging, the other vandalized items, everything. Other than fear and anger, nothing jumped out at her.

Ten minutes later, Maggie arrived, checked out the aisle, the box and the cut wires then suggested Steph might want to close the store itself. Darcy could keep doing business outside.

Steph fought the urge to cry; she couldn't afford any weakness these days. Instead, she had to stay strong and determined if she was going to pull through this siege. Because that was how she was coming to see what was happening to her. She felt battered—repeatedly—as if she were under nonstop attack, an attack against which she was powerless.

Shortly after Maggie arrived, Hal Benson strode into the store for the second time that day. "What happened this time?"

Blinking hard to keep the tears from welling, Steph pointed to the box of litter. "You might call it tampering. I call it destroying. And criminal." She showed him the cut wires.

For the next twenty minutes, Maggie and Hal went through the routine that was becoming painfully familiar—they looked at everything, hit her with a million questions.

"There's no way you could come up with a list of today's customers, is there?" Hal asked.

"Are you kidding?" She glanced at the shoppers milling around the tables out on the sidewalk, walking in and out of the other stores, as well as the curiosity seekers peering in her front window. "There are tons of people out there, the same tons of people who've been in and out all day long. My register hasn't stopped ringing since I opened up."

Maggie came over, a frown pleating her brow, a dusting of black powder on her right sleeve. "I would have been surprised if we'd gotten any decent prints from the box or the shelf. But I had to give it a shot."

"I understand," Steph said. "What's next?"

Maggie and Hal exchanged looks. Hal then turned to Steph, while Maggie packed up her fingerprint kit.

"I think you should close up," Maggie said. "At least for the rest of the afternoon."

"Why?" Steph asked, dismayed at the thought of even more lost business. "The box is ruined, and Maggie even checked for prints already. I don't think whoever did it is going to come back. I'm sure they know you guys have been here. Besides, it was just a box of kitty litter. No missing drugs this time."

"We'd rather you kept the place locked up until you get the surveillance set up again. And you might want to look into a more sophisticated system, one without such obvious wiring. That way we can keep track of comings and goings. I can meet you here when you have the security company come in," Hal offered. "Maybe on Monday."

A security company. Great. Visions of fleeing dollars danced in her head. "With the added cost of a new system, I'd like to stay open until the end of the day."

Hal and Maggie traded looks. "How late were you planning to stay open? Five? Six? It's not that much longer."

"Six." She caught her bottom lip between her teeth. "But if I do close, I'll lose even more money. I had to close down the Saturday of the break-in, and I've had product loss like never before…"

She stopped. Her words were having no effect on either cop. "Okay. Fine. I'll get Darcy and Jimmy to start bringing everything back in. It's really not that much earlier in the greater scheme of things." A surge of anger at her situation flared up. "Either one of you want to hang around to keep an eye on me as I close up?"

The blush on Hal's cheeks was gratifying; Maggie's sheepish shrug fell into the irritating category.

"Follow me," Steph said.

While Darcy and Jimmy put away the products from the outside booth and cleaned up the spilled litter, Steph continued to ring up sales. But her mind wasn't really in her work. Who'd had access to those wires?

Well, on a day like this, just about anyone.

"Missy!" Mabel Sowers, a widow with a deep, carrying voice, rapped her knuckles on the pharmacy counter. "You gotta pay attention here. You gave me someone else's stuff."

Steph gasped. "I'm so sorry, Mrs. Sowers. It won't happen again."

And it couldn't. She wouldn't let her attention drift again.

She glanced through the front window and saw Darcy folding one of the tables, while Jimmy carried in the rest of the products they'd arranged outside. Good. They were almost finished.

Once they were done, she went through every last step of her routine, Officer Lowe at her heels, Hal right behind. By that time, it was close to five thirty. At least she would only lose about a half hour's worth of business this time.

Hal said goodbye. To her surprise, Maggie insisted on following Steph out to her car—this late in the fall, dusk came early, and it was getting dark. Steph couldn't quite bring herself to argue against the company.

But while on the back steps of the store, Maggie's cell phone rang. After a handful of answers, she turned to Steph, an apologetic look on her face.

"Sorry. I have to go. A three-car pileup, and Wayne needs my help." She shook her head. "Can't wait until we hire at least one more officer."

"Go ahead. I'll be fine." She hoped. "And I'll pray for that officer to happen soon."

"Thanks!"

As Maggie ran off, a ripple of fear ran through Steph. But

she couldn't give in to the feeling. How different could it be, walking to her car without the policewoman at her side? Nothing had changed, just the comfort she'd gained from the company.

She still always had her Lord at her side. She would lean on Him.

Praying, she crossed the side street. As she did, she heard a soft crunch of footsteps behind her. She darted a look over her shoulder but saw nothing, so she kept on going, figuring she'd imagined the sounds.

Although she heard nothing else, at least not nearby, since Main Street still rang with the sounds of many festival attendees, Steph couldn't shake the sense that someone was out there, that she wasn't the only one on the shadowed and empty street. She could almost feel the person's gaze in a physical way.

Squaring her shoulders, she came to a decision. Whatever kind of surveillance system she had installed, it would have to cover the alley as well as the store.

She hated the hyperawareness of a strange presence, so she sped up. When she reached the rental's driver-side door and took her car key from her pants pocket, Steph again felt phantom fingers crawl up her neck. Looking in all directions, behind her, to either side, peering into the shadows around the corner of the fabric store, in the delivery doorway of the empty bookstore, under the video store's awning and next to the unlike Loganton New Age store, Steph saw no one. With a shaky breath, she clicked the lock button, sat, clicked again and turned the key in the ignition.

By the time she'd driven a couple of blocks, however, her hands shook so hard she could hardly keep the car on the road. With a quick prayer for strength, she pulled into the next parking lot she saw.

Clearly an answer to prayer. She hadn't really registered

where she was, but somehow she'd managed to pull into Loganton Bible Church property.

As familiar as it felt to be there, since this was the church her family had attended for generations, Steph still couldn't shake her fear. With trembling fingers, she dug into her purse and grabbed her phone. When Hal Benson answered, she let out a shaky breath.

"S-someone was watching…when I left the store…"

"Where are you now?"

She tried to speak but her voice broke, so she thought of the God who loved her, protected her, and then gained enough composure to try again. In spits and spurts, she gave Hal a handful of details. Then, when she felt she couldn't say another word, he told her to stay put. He'd meet her in less than five minutes.

"Good," she whispered. "I don't think…I doubt I can move."

But in her condition, she was easy prey.

EIGHT

Steph counted the seconds until a pair of headlights pulled into the church parking lot. The car's arrival brought relief. That was immediately followed by more fear. Was it Hal?

Another set of lights made the turn seconds later. The first car spun its wheels, took the turn at the end of the parking lot apron too fast and sped away down the street. As it disappeared, Steph realized it was too dark for her to have registered even the color or make of the car.

The second car backed up and took after the first, but by the time it reached the street, the first vehicle had disappeared. It pulled back into the parking lot and came parallel to Steph's car.

Her heart pounded. Should she try to leave? Was this Hal? Who had the other driver been?

With shaking fingers, she checked her door locks. Good. They were down. But if this driver came armed with a gun, a locked door wouldn't do her any good. She did the only thing she could. She prayed. Again.

Only when she heard a light tap on her window did Steph open her eyes. Hal was peering in. She exhaled, realizing she'd been holding her breath.

"Are you okay?" he asked once she stood beside him.

"I think so. But what about the other car?"

He shook his head, a frustrated look on his face. "There's no point trying to follow. I didn't see where he turned. Did you get a look at whoever followed you?"

The simple but obvious question made Steph feel stupid. "Um…well, I never did see anyone. I just…just *felt* them—a presence. You know. It was that creepy feeling up the back of your neck when someone's watching you."

"I see…"

From the way he said the two words, Steph wondered if he really did see anything. But she lacked the courage to say another word.

He went on. "You *sensed* someone…what? Following you? Watching you?"

"Definitely watching me. And then, that car pulled in a few minutes after I did. The one that sped right by you."

"The one in a mighty hurry to get out of here."

"That one."

For a moment, Hal stared in the direction the car had taken. Then he doffed his hat, smacked it against his leg and finally met her gaze. "Can't deny that car left the minute I drove the county car—with its county seal—into the parking lot. It could have just needed to turn around. But it could have followed you, too."

Steph tipped up her chin. "That was an awfully fast retreat, if you ask me. But I guess we'll never know, will we?"

"We will once we catch whoever broke into your store."

"True." She bit her bottom lip. After a second, she chided herself for her cowardice. She had to be able to ask the man a question. He wasn't about to clap handcuffs on her and haul her away for something like that. "So tell me, Sheriff Benson. Do you believe you'll actually catch someone? Other than me, that is."

She held her breath, waiting for his response. His answer mattered, probably more than it should.

"Yeah," he drawled. "I suppose I do. Police work's not fast or glamorous, but we usually do take care of business. And as far as you're concerned...well, let's just say something about that rock and its threat on your windshield and that car that just tore out of here leads me to think you're in the clear."

"Now there's a ringing endorsement."

It was his turn to shrug. "It comes with the job. I don't work in absolutes until the evidence is in and the crook's behind bars."

"I can't fault you for that." She looked around the dark, empty lot. "Looks like the danger's gone now. I can head home—"

"Not so fast. I want you to take me back to where you first 'felt' someone watching you. I'd like to see if they left any sign of having been there."

Steph scoffed. "Sure. Like they left colored Post-its in the pharmacy for you to follow and find. Why would you expect them to get careless all of a sudden?"

"I'm not sure that's what I expect, but it doesn't hurt to check. You never know what you'll find unless you look."

She shook her head. The granite line of his jaw showed his determination. "Okay, then. Let's get going."

As she turned toward her car, Hal caught her arm. The warmth of his touch surprised her. The gentleness of his clasp pleased her. The comfort of his company startled her.

"Wait," he said. "Why don't you come with me? It doesn't make sense to have to find two parking spots on an evening when downtown's packed."

Steph stared as his long, strong fingers slid down to hold her wrist loosely. She slanted a glance at his face and realized he, too, was staring at their point of contact. The reality of the circumstances hit her then. They were all alone in a parking lot. Hal was twice her size. And yet…she felt safer right then than she had since the night of the mugging.

Seconds crawled by. Hal looked up and met her gaze. His touch went through a very subtle shift then, and it felt more like a caress than a grip. She'd always known how attractive Hal was, but now she knew more. She knew how dedicated he was, how generous with his time, how caring, even putting up with Granny Annie's antics.

It struck her how much she wanted him to believe her, how much she wanted him to like her. Because, as crazy as it was, she not only admired and respected the sheriff but she also liked the man she was coming to know.

"Steph—"

Headlights from a passing car pierced her gaze, breaking the closeness, the connection between her and Hal. He dropped her arm as though it burned.

Reality crashed down on her again. After all, they *were* in a parking lot, next to a church where construction equipment lay dormant until Monday morning, she still felt besieged, and they hadn't yet caught the person who'd stolen the pseudoephedrine from her store. This was no time to entertain fantasies of budding romance. Or something like that.

"Er…we—ah…we'd better get going," Hal said, his voice a bit rough.

Embarrassed, Steph nodded, unable to speak. She grabbed her purse from the passenger seat of her car, clicked the lock remote and got into Hal's official vehicle. He started up the engine, put the car in Reverse and they pulled out into the street.

Moments later, the radio crackled to life. The dispatcher rattled off details about a number of deputies' assignments. Hal "uh-huhed" a handful of times, then suggested someone take off early. As they turned into the alley behind Scott's Pharmacy, the woman on the other end said, "10-4, Sheriff."

"Oh, and I'm going off duty," Hal added.

"On the stump again?"

"You got it."

"See ya at the high school then."

"I'm sorry," Steph said when he signed off. "I didn't realize you had a campaign event scheduled. Really. You don't have to babysit me. Maybe I imagined the person following me. You should go ahead with your plans."

By the glow of the single light post at the mouth of the alley, Steph saw him arch a brow. "Like you imagined the car I saw fly by me in the parking lot? Like you imagined the stolen drugs? And the mugger? I guess if you ignore the cut wires on the cameras, then the jury's still out on the artistically altered boxes on your shelves."

"You have a point. But those times there was something to see—or after the break-in, something *not* to see." She got out. "Look. I'll call Darcy to give me a ride home. Your constituents are probably waiting for you." She pasted on a bright smile. "And you don't want Granny to come chase you down with a wooden spoon!"

As lame as her attempt at humor was, he still laughed. "Trust me. I don't do anything to get on Granny's bad side—I like to eat, you know. But look. Something scared you enough to call me. It's worth taking a few minutes to check things out. Besides, aren't you one of my constituents, too?"

She smiled. "Sure am. But I'm also the one keeping you away from the campaign. If you insist on checking out what I'm beginning to think was nothing more than my imagi-

We'd like to send you two free books to introduce you to the Love Inspired® Suspense series. These books are worth over $10, but are yours to keep absolutely FREE! We'll even send you two wonderful surprise gifts. You can't lose!

Each of your **FREE** books is filled with riveting inspirational suspense featuring Christian characters facing challenges to their faith...and their lives!

GET 2 FREE BOOKS!

HURRY!
Return this card today to get 2 FREE Books and 2 FREE Bonus Gifts!

YES! Please send me the **2 FREE Love Inspired® Suspense books** and **2 FREE gifts** for which I qualify. I understand that I am under no obligation to purchase anything further, as explained on the back of this card.

Love Inspired®
SUSPENSE
RIVETING INSPIRATIONAL ROMANCE

PLACE
FREE GIFTS
SEAL HERE

▲ DETACH AND MAIL CARD TODAY! ▲

LISUSR-IV-08

323 IDL ERRH   123 IDL ERQT

FIRST NAME

LAST NAME

ADDRESS

APT.#   CITY

STATE/PROV.   ZIP/POSTAL CODE

Steeple Hill Reader Service — Here's How It Works:

Accepting your 2 free books and 2 free mystery gifts places you under no obligation to buy anything. You may keep the books and gifts and return the shipping statement marked "cancel." If you do not cancel, about a month later we'll send you 4 additional books and bill you just $4.24 each in the U.S. or $4.74 each in Canada, plus 25¢ shipping & handling per book and applicable taxes if any.* That's the complete price — and at a savings of at least 15% off the cover price, it's quite a bargain! You may cancel at any time, but if you choose to continue, every month we'll send you 4 more books, which you may either purchase at the discount price or return to us and cancel your subscription.

*Terms and prices subject to change without notice. Sales tax applicable in N.Y. Canadian residents will be charged applicable provincial taxes and GST. Offer not valid in Quebec. All orders subject to approval. Books received may not be as shown. Credit or debit balances in a customer's account(s) may be offset by any other outstanding balance owed by or to the customer. Please allow 4 to 6 weeks for delivery. Offer available while quantities last.

If offer card is missing write to:

Steeple Hill Reader Service, 3010 Walden Ave., P.O. Box 1867, Buffalo, NY 14240-1867

BUSINESS REPLY MAIL
FIRST-CLASS MAIL   PERMIT NO. 717   BUFFALO, NY

POSTAGE WILL BE PAID BY ADDRESSEE

STEEPLE HILL READER SERVICE
3010 WALDEN AVE
PO BOX 1867
BUFFALO NY 14240-9952

NO POSTAGE
NECESSARY
IF MAILED
IN THE
UNITED STATES

nation, then you'd better get going. You won't get much from a campaign event for a gone-home crowd."

He pulled a flashlight from behind the driver's seat and beamed it at the ground. To Steph, it seemed more than futile. "It's dark. I doubt you'll see anything out here."

He shrugged but kept peering into the shadows. Steph watched, arms crossed, the sounds from Main Street snagging her attention from time to time. By now, the booths had probably been taken down since the rest of the festivities would take place at the high-school gym.

When Hal turned off the flashlight, the darkness caught Steph by surprise. "Are you done?" she asked.

"As I can be for tonight."

"Do you think you'll find something more in the morning?"

"I don't know. Won't know until I check then."

While she'd watched Hal inspect every possible inch of alley space, the sidewalks and the street she'd crossed to the lot where she parked her car during the workday, Steph had sold herself on the idea that her imagination had overtaken her common sense. After all, she did have a lively imagination, and the litter-box incident had made her jumpy.

She tried to do the same with Hal. He considered it then nodded. "Could be, but we can't be too careful. You've already been attacked twice. I want to avoid a third."

A shudder ran through her. "I hadn't really thought of it that way, but I suppose you're right."

"I don't know how else you could consider it."

"I've kept the two events separate in my mind, but it makes sense to connect them."

"And that's why I think it would be a good thing if I were to follow you out to your place."

"But you have a campaign event—"

"Why don't you come with me? Once I'm done with my speech, we can go retrieve your car. Did you…um…have any…er…plans for the evening?"

The suddenly stammering sheriff seemed inordinately interested in her response. Did he think she had a heist of her own store planned for the evening?

Then another possibility occurred to her. She remembered Hal's awkwardness when he'd asked her to join him for a cup of coffee at the diner. She also remembered—who could forget?—the special moment they'd just shared out at the church parking lot. Was his interest personal?

In either case, she was at Hal's mercy now. She had no way to get home until he took her back to her car. While she'd always thought of Loganton as quiet and safe, and she loved to walk down its tree-lined streets, no way would she even consider going the four blocks to the church by foot. Not now; not after the trouble at the store, in the dark and especially not with so many people—strangers—out and about.

"Okay, Sheriff. I guess I could do double duty and help your campaign manager hand out literature while you give your speech. Knowing her, Granny Annie won't want anyone to leave this year's Fall Fest without a flyer with your name on it."

He made a strangled sound somewhere between a choke and a groan. "Don't remind me. I have to wonder if I took her on in a flash of wisdom or a flare of weakened willpower."

Steph laughed. "Hey, you could do worse. Granny's honest, she's hardworking, she cares and she knows a ton of people. How could you lose?"

"I don't want to think about it. It was all those people she knows I was thinking of when I took her on board." He headed back to the cruiser. "Let's go. She's going to chew me out as it is."

By the time they reached the high-school gym, it seemed everyone else in town and beyond had decided to do the same. Hal grasped Steph's elbow to lead her through the crowd, and she again grew too aware of his presence at her side. She'd never responded to a man like that before. True, she'd never been interested in fly-by-night romance or dating for the sake of dating, but if a man had ever come by who'd affected her like Hal Benson was affecting her, she would have noticed.

Less than ten steps inside the building, however, Granny Annie spotted them and marched right over.

"This is wonderful!" She hugged Steph and winked at Hal. "It's awful good to see the both of you're not back to eating supper all by your lonesomes tonight. Make sure you have yourselves all the sloppy joes you can eat over at my booth. Tell Karla they're on the house today."

Granny held a monopoly—and the county fair blue ribbon—on the sloppy joe venture. Steph's mouth began to water. "I can't turn down one of those."

"Well, you just go on ahead and eat. The sheriff and I—" Granny V'ed the index and middle fingers of her hand, pointed them at her twinkly eyes then at Hal, and back to her eyes again "—have to have us a meetin' of the minds." She leaned toward Steph. "Is that eye thing not the coolest thing? I saw it on cable TV the other night."

Steph laughed. "You're cool, all right."

Then Granny shoved another fistful of flyers at her. "Hand 'em out for us, will ya?"

Before Steph could react, Granny dragged Hal away. Steph stood for a moment, staring at them, then at the papers. She'd suggested the possibility to Hal, mostly as a joke. But how had she let Granny Annie rope her into campaigning for Hal? The woman was a force unto herself. And Steph had better get on with the business of "politicking" for the sheriff if she didn't want to wind up on the older woman's wrong side.

She gave the next person she saw a brilliant smile and held out a paper. "Here. Make sure you vote Hal Benson for sheriff."

Her first victim, Rosalie Watkins, a nurse at the hospital, gave Steph a puzzled look. "I don't get it," she said. "You're campaigning for the man who hasn't caught the guy who broke into your store?"

"He's working on it." Steph winced. Even to her own ears, her defense sounded weak. "I trust Sheriff Benson."

The nurse tapped her nose with the campaign literature. "You know…I've been hearing whispers about writing in that Ethan Rodgers for sheriff. He's the one who used to be a DEA agent up in Chicago? He did find that drug lab not so long ago."

"But I thought he was recovering from a serious gunshot wound. I don't think he'd be up to the job."

"He won't be recovering forever."

"B-but he's also getting ready for a wedding. Isn't that coming soon? He's not thinking election these days, you know."

"Oh, he can start the job once he's married. The election's scheduled for right after his honeymoon."

Steph shook her head. "Sheriff Benson's the right man."

"If you say so." Rosalie didn't sound convinced.

As the nurse strolled away, Steph couldn't shake the feeling she'd failed in her politicking efforts. Poor Hal. Not only did he have to go up against that obnoxious Ed Townsend but it looked like he would also have to beat a former drug enforcement expert who wasn't even running. And all because Steph hadn't been able to keep the meds under lock and key.

She had to do something. If it were the last thing she did that night, she would find a good home for all the handouts Granny Annie had given her.

On her mission, Steph chatted up neighbors she hadn't seen in weeks. While most were enthusiastic supporters of the sheriff, a few had moved on to Ed's column. An even smaller percentage had joined the write-in-Ethan-for-sheriff camp, a situation that bothered her.

Steph had nothing against Ethan Rodgers. She hardly knew him, but she did know he had a stellar reputation, a career gilded with a ton of awards and the good sense to fall in love with Tess Graver. But he wasn't the sheriff. He wasn't Hal.

Then came the speeches. The mayor introduced Ed first. The lawyer pontificated far longer than Steph thought anyone could have without saying anything of substance. But then again, it was Ed. What really infuriated her, though, was the dump-Hal-who's-no-good tone he adopted right from the start. By the time he finally wound up his comments, Steph's jaw hurt from biting down to keep from arguing against his snide remarks.

Then the mayor introduced Hal. In calm tones, he outlined his vision for the county. He spoke of cooperation between his office and the local police departments. He spoke of community programs to cut down on DUI arrests. He outlined programs to alert kids to Stranger Danger. Most of all, he spoke of his commitment to erasing drug crime from his jurisdiction.

Hal described a multipronged program that started with building an alliance between parents, law enforcement and the schools. He planned to add additional patrols for areas where kids gathered and drug pushers trolled, and he wound up his proposal by pledging support to individual police departments in their efforts to hire more officers.

Before he even reached the midway point in his speech, Steph's respect for the man had mushroomed into something else. She didn't have a word to describe the cross between awe and admiration she felt for Hal. And she couldn't ignore the warmth and attraction that underlined those other feelings. She just knew she couldn't let her problems get in the way of Hal's reelection.

To a healthy burst of applause, Hal waved his thanks to the crowd, ran down the stage steps and then made straight for Steph.

"That was fantastic!" she said when he reached her side.

He grimaced. "That was murder."

"What do you mean?"

"Let's get some food."

"Food's wonderful," she said, "but we're going to talk, too."

"If you insist." When she frowned, he grinned. "Okay, I promise."

With his agreement ringing in her ears, Steph led them to the sloppy joe booth. After waiting patiently at the end of the long line, they scored heaping plates of tangy sandwiches, creamy potato salad and crisp carrots and celery sticks. Armed with their food and tall cups of iced tea, they left the gym in search of a quieter dining area.

They found what they were looking for in a corner of the school's front lobby. A pair of folding chairs had been left leaning against a wall, and while Steph held the plates, Hal set them up. They laughed, they ate, they talked.

Steph was stunned to learn of Hal's shyness, while he looked surprised when she told him how tough her learning disability had made her life. She was thrilled when he told her of his grandfather, who'd risen through the ranks to become chief in Atlanta, the man who'd inspired him to go into law enforcement instead of academia. They discussed the campaign, and Steph let Hal know how sorry she was her troubles were affecting his reelection. That led them to dissect the case.

"No one's ever suspected me of any kind of wrongdoing before," she said. "It's the worst feeling. Especially, since I've worked so hard to make the store a success. I'm not into drugs, nor would I ever involve myself with anyone who is."

"I know."

"Excuse me?"

"I said, I know. Someone's after the pseudoephedrine, but it's not you."

The tension that had held Steph in a vise grip ever since the night of the mugging drained from every inch of her body. The reprieve was so intense that she sagged against the chair. Tears welled in her eyes.

"Are you okay?" Hal asked, leaning close, a hand on her chair's metal back.

She nodded. One lone tear spilled down her cheek. "I'm glad you don't think I…stole the drugs. How anyone would think I'd do anything to hurt the people I've worked so hard to help, I'll never know. Besides, I'd never jeopardize my license, even though it's already been jeopardized."

He looked away.

"You know the PD had to notify the DEA. Then they had to notify the Bureau of Pharmacy Services, which now has no choice but to launch an investigation."

Could an already crummy day get any worse? The moment the thought crossed Steph's mind, she shut it down. Of course, things could get worse. She could actually lose her license. Her business could go belly-up. One of her parents could get hurt—

"Oh, no!" She rubbed her eyes, drying up the tears. She had too much to do to give in to crying. "I'd better get to Mom and Dad before they hear about all this from friends or, worse, the newspaper."

"You mean you haven't told them? How could they not know?"

"Well, they live just outside Charlotte now, and they don't come out to Loganton all that often anymore. And I sure didn't run to them with all the ugly details."

"I'd let them in on what's happening if I were you."

Steph bit down on her bottom lip then nodded. "That's going to be one fun conversation."

"Do you want company?"

The moment he said the words, Steph saw him wince. She smiled. "I guess your mouth got the better of your thoughts there, didn't it?"

He gave her a sheepish grin. "But I'm sticking by the offer. If you want my help, I'm there. And you can count on my help on the rest of what's been happening, too."

She studied his face and again recognized how much she'd come to like the sheriff. "What do you mean? You're already working my case."

A wash of red swept up his face. "Um, not...exactly."

"What do you mean?"

He turned away. "It's not really my jurisdiction. But I...ah...take the drug problem seriously...in the county. You understand."

"Are you telling me this isn't your job?"

"Not really." He ran a hand through his hair. "But I do want to help. I want to help you put an end to what's going on. And I want to put the drug dealer behind bars. You can count on my help anytime."

A wave of guilt washed over Steph. "Oh, no. You really shouldn't worry about my mess. That wouldn't be right. I'm sure Officers Donnelly and Lowe will get the thief. I couldn't ask you to—"

"You didn't ask. I offered. I'm just thinking that a little extra effort might put an end to the siege and move things along to a resolution." A slow smile brightened his face. "Besides, you know what they say about two heads being better than one. Maybe if we put our heads together we'll find something we missed before."

As awkward as she felt, she also was relieved. She'd felt so alone ever since the night she was mugged. "If you're sure."

He nodded.

"Then that's good enough for me—"

"Be seein' ya, Sheriff," the mayor called out as he herded his wife and two daughters out of the school.

Hal tapped his forehead in a salute then turned back to Steph. But before he said anything else, a large cluster of Fest-goers headed out. They all had a goodbye for Hal, Steph or both.

By the time a third group departed, she realized more than politeness and good manners spurred the farewells. The sharp curiosity in the Logantonians' demeanor gave them away. Loganton was, after all, a small town. When two of its more visible residents were spotted huddled together in a dim corner, the collective interest was spiked.

"Uh-oh," she said. "You're in trouble now."

"What do you mean?"

"The gossips are going to keep the phones busy once they get home. By morning, you'll either have arrested me or be hog-tied to me, according to the worst rumors."

He gave her a long stare and then smiled a very interested, very male smile. "Trust me. I can use the positive press. Having my name linked to yours doesn't bother me one bit. In fact, I welcome the connection."

Steph got the feeling he was saying more than what she voiced, but she quickly stifled the spark of pleasure the thought lit. "You might come to regret being linked to a crime suspect, especially in the middle of the campaign."

"Not to worry." His words echoed the confidence she saw in his face. "We're going to catch this guy and clear your name. It's a win-win for me. What man wouldn't want to be in my place? You, Stephanie Scott, are one lovely lady."

Steph dragged in a sharp breath. Oh, my! And to think she'd never seen the sheriff in the role of romantic hero. Could a man be a practical, nitty-gritty kind of guy *and* fit into her romantic dreams?

There was only one way to know, and she was in the perfect position to find out. "Partners in crime, then," she murmured.

"Crime-busters," he countered.

Both smiled.

NINE

Hal watched Steph get into her car, unable to stifle his wry smile. He had all the courage necessary when it came to his job, but when it came to one Stephanie Scott? That's when the word *wimp* came to mind.

But he'd found a way to get around his nerves; he'd found the perfect way to spend more time with her. Well, if he were totally honest about it, he'd have to admit she'd been the one to come up with the idea. But he was no fool. He knew a great opportunity when one walked up to him.

There was no denying she needed this sorry mess resolved. He'd had his doubts about her part in it at first, but as he'd proceeded with the investigation and gotten to know her better, his instincts had told him she wasn't the kind of person who would let herself be lured into the dangerous trap of drug crime. He *knew* Steph was innocent. And knowing how much was at stake for her, he also knew he couldn't stop until she was in the clear.

They both faced losing the careers they loved.

Steph flashed her headlights as she drove past him. He flashed back then pulled up to the curb behind her. As she turned the corner, he drove out, heading in the opposite direction, his mind on their dilemma.

A fair number of voters were beginning to listen to Ed's insinuations and outright accusations, even though no one was taking that campaign very seriously. Hal also knew the Ethan Rodgers write-in campaign was gaining strength. If he didn't put Steph's vandal/mugger/drug thief/rock thrower behind bars soon, he'd be attending Ethan's swearing-in ceremony and passing him the reins.

Only one problem: he had no clues. Truth be told, Hal wasn't sure he was dealing with only one person. Logic told him Steph was being targeted because of the drugs she kept behind the counter. Last time he checked, though, the justice system needed more than his gut feeling or an attack of logic to put someone away.

He glanced at the clock on his dash. Steph was probably pulling into her cute little place. It had surprised him to see such a no-nonsense person like the town's pretty pharmacist living in such a frilly, ultrafeminine nest. And since Steph was supposed to be safely inside that nest, he was going to swing by and make sure.

As he approached the carriage house, a light went on in her small living room. Through the curtains he could just make out her silhouette. She paused, leaned forward—probably turning on the small TV—then straightened and ran a hand through her short, choppy-cut blond hair.

A powerful urge to run his fingers through the soft, tousled strands rocked him.

But she was inside; he was outside. So instead, he went home. Alone.

Steph turned on the news when she walked into her living room. Exhaustion hit her, and the frequent dull throb at the base of her spine cranked it up a notch. She ran a hand through her hair as she pressed her other fist into the sweet spot of pain.

As the newscaster babbled on, the loneliness threatened to overwhelm her. By comparison, eating with Hal Benson in the school lobby had been a rare treat. He was great company. They hadn't run out of things to talk about that whole time, even though they'd sat there for over two hours. As tall, quiet and down-to-earth as he was, she'd discovered the sheriff hid a healthy sense of humor behind the surprising shyness. They'd laughed time and time again over his clever insights into details, people and events. And yet, he carried with him an air of command and strength, and Steph appreciated knowing she could trust him.

In her situation, she needed someone to trust.

Who'd have thought the ultrastudious valedictorian from high school would have gone into law enforcement instead of rocket science or a professorship in the ivory tower of academia? Not her. Still, Steph understood what a bonus Hal's intelligence was when added to his training and years of experience.

If she were to protect her hard-won reputation as a reliable pharmacist, she would need every bit of smarts, knowledge and the solid track record Hal had racked up over the years.

And if she was perfectly honest, it wasn't just the tangibles she appreciated. There was something about Hal Benson…

During the time she'd spent with him she'd felt attractive, interesting and very, very feminine.

And he hadn't uttered a single romantic word.

Who would have thought?

Monday evening, after she took care of the last stragglers, Steph locked up Scott's and then headed for church. She'd joined the women's evening Bible study as soon as she returned to Loganton to open up her brand-new drugstore. After five years of digging into the Word with them, she'd come to know the eclectic group of women like sisters and aunts, and she couldn't imagine life without a support group like hers.

The usual volume of chitchat greeted her as she walked into the classroom.

"Hi, Steph!"

"Hey, how's the store these days?"

"There you are!" Miss Tabitha Cranston, Darcy's employer, called out. "Did you hear my Bootsy had her kittens? You'll be able to take one of those sweet babies home with you in about four weeks."

Half of Steph wanted a kitten. The other half told her she was crazy to even consider pet ownership with her schedule. But today, the memory of the weekend's loneliness loomed large. Still… "I'm not sure it's the best idea, Miss Tabitha. I work such long hours, and I'd hate to leave a kitty alone for so much time every day."

Miss Tabitha slipped her arm around Steph's waist, and together they walked toward the table in the center of the room. "That's the beauty of cat ownership, honey. I'm telling you, I now wish I'd gotten a cat years ago. They don't need anywhere near as much fussing as dogs do. Have you heard all the trouble Gordon's niece's crazy little mutt is making over there? That little scamp of a pooch won't even let Tess's fiancé come near him…"

As the two women waited for the class's leader to call them to prayer, Miss Tabitha elaborated on the pet problems plaguing the former DEA agent and his soon-to-be wife.

Steph listened, gleaning details about the man's recovery from the serious gunshot wound he'd sustained when he'd brought a drug dealer to justice. But between details of the risky surgeries followed by grueling therapy, the occasional stare aimed her way snagged her attention. She smiled, but each one of the women she caught staring immediately averted her gaze without a responding smile.

Hmm...

During the class, the measuring looks continued coming her way. By the time everyone chimed in on the closing "Amen," Steph felt as though she'd regressed back to elementary school, as if someone had stuck a sign on her back. Even at this age, she hated not being in on the message it told.

Of course, she was probably the object of everyone's attention because of all the problems she'd been having at the pharmacy. Did even these women think she'd had something to do with the theft of the pseudoephedrine?

How? How could women she'd prayed with, cried with and rejoiced with suspect her? Hadn't they come to know her better than that? If they suspected her, did they also question her competence? After all, she hadn't been able to prevent the theft.

On her way out, Winnie Zook, owner of the knitting supplies store a few doors from the drugstore, hurried up to Steph. "I didn't realize you knew the sheriff that well," the well-known gossip said. "You make one fine couple."

Steph's cheeks burned. "Oh, no, Winnie. We're not a couple. We were just discussing the case. I'm sure you know all about the break-in at my place."

Winnie gave an exaggerated shudder. "Of course, I know. And I'll tell you, I've been scared stupid ever since. I wind up checking my locks over and over and over again. Has that Hal of yours caught the thief yet?"

Great. What did she tackle first? Did she refute the "Hal

of yours" part or did she give her stock "he's working on it and making progress" response? Neither one felt right; she didn't think she'd get anywhere in either case.

"I'm sure you're fine at your place," is what she opted for.

"Maybe, but no one else knows that. And it might scare them away from coming downtown. Where'll I be then?"

Although Winnie had framed the question with regards to her own store, Steph had often wondered how this spate of criminal activity would affect Scott's Pharmacy. She couldn't afford a drop in business, and the suspicion of her fellow Logantonians could harm her store far more than the vandal ever had.

"See?" Winnie said. "You're thinking the same thing I was."

Steph couldn't just come out and deny the charge, since she had a natural aversion to lies. Even fudging gave her heartburn. "I'm sure Sheriff Benson and the Loganton PD will have things cleared up in no time. Certainly before our businesses suffer."

"Oh, I don't know…Rosalie says what we need is someone with *real* experience." Winnie's chocolate-brown eyes were wide with alarm. "And Abby Diller says the right man for the job isn't Sheriff Benson or that silly Ed Townsend, either. She says Ethan Rodgers is the man for us. He must've busted more druggies in one year than Hal Benson will in his whole life. Experience counts. And he did log in all those years with the DEA in Chicago, you know."

Oh, Steph knew. She knew too well. But she disagreed. "I don't see what anyone can have against Sheriff Benson. He's doing an outstanding job, helping the Loganton PD with the investigation even though he doesn't have to. Besides, I don't think Mr. Rodgers has any interest in returning to law enforcement. He came here to retire."

Cora Tibbs, a friend of Steph's mother, came up and

hugged her. "Now, honey. Tell me all that's happening with you and that handsome rascal sheriff of yours. He's so quiet…but I hear tell silent waters run deep. Must be."

Winnie crossed her arms and donned a smug smile.

Steph blushed—again. "Miss Tibbs, the sheriff and I are only acquaintances. We were discussing the case last night at the Fest."

The former librarian winked. "Oh, sure. I see, I see." Then, nodding in a maddening way, she trotted off, ready to tote her tale to the next willing ear.

Steph had had enough. "I have to head home now," she told the now smirking Winnie. "I'll see you next week."

Hours later, once she'd crawled into bed with her Bible, Steph turned to the Lord in prayer. "Please, Father, protect Hal. Don't let what's happened to me rob him of the job he loves so much. Which could happen, now that everyone's started to link him to me."

As she whispered the words, a parallel thought crossed her mind.

Please don't let a drug dealer rob me of the store I love so much, either. More than just me, he'd be robbing everyone in town of something they all need as much as I do, if in a different way.

She placed the Holy Book on her nightstand, turned off her light and turned on her side. A tear rolled from her eye into the hair at her temple.

That's when she wished Miss Tabitha's kittens had been old enough so she could have brought one home.

When Steph went to the garage the next morning, horror socked her right in the gut. Someone had been there. She had no idea how they'd gotten in, since the automatic opener locked the door as it brought it down, but the evidence was undeniable. All four of her tires had been slashed.

She couldn't get to work.

When she dialed for help, she asked for the police officers to head straight for the store. "I'm afraid whoever did this wanted to keep me away. Once the officers are done checking the pharmacy, they can come and look at my tires. I'll go wait for them at the feed store, since I don't really feel like staying here alone."

The dispatcher reminded her to touch as little as possible and to keep an eye out for the patrol car.

As if she could have made herself do anything else. She would count the seconds until help came.

On her way to the busy supply store a handful of yards away from her carriage house, Steph wondered if Hal had been in his cruiser when she'd called for help. Had she heard the dispatcher? Would he come? Or should she call him?

Yes, she was coming to rely on him, far more than she would have expected, and maybe more than she should. But she really liked talking to him, watching his brilliant mind work on the puzzle before them. He'd offered to help her, to catch the thief and put him behind bars, but Steph feared continued contact with her, especially since everyone in town now knew they'd eaten together at the Fest, would only do him harm. This was the worst possible time for her to fall for the sheriff.

The last thing Hal Benson needed as he ran for reelection was a woman under a cloud of suspicion.

Sure enough, the pharmacy had been broken into again—ransacked, this time, and cleaned of all controlled substances. Hal hadn't hesitated when Wayne called him. "I'll be there."

"We have it under control. You really don't have to haul yourself out here. I just figured you'd want to know."

"How's Steph?"

"She's fine. Her bank account's a whole lot lighter, seeing as she'll be needing four new tires, not to mention everything they busted in the pharmacy to get to the drugs, but it could have been much worse. She was sleeping upstairs when it all came down."

Hal felt sick. "Is she still home? Or did she insist on going to the store?"

"She's at the store. Got that nutty Darcy to give her a ride in that piece of junk of hers."

"I'll run by and see how Steph's doing. She's got to be pretty scared."

"Mad's more like it. Never seen that little girl anything other'n smiling, but today? Today nobody better get on her nerves. She'll tear right into them."

"Do you blame her?"

"Not one bit."

"Thanks for calling."

"No big deal. See ya."

Hal was sure it was a big deal for Steph.

By the time he reached the store, she was locking up. She'd hung a small rectangular sign on the door proclaiming the place closed, even though it wasn't much past one o'clock, in the front window. The night of the Fest she'd confided how near to the edge of trouble she ran the business, and he knew the loss of revenue would worry her.

Worse yet, she'd be scared of going home. With good reason.

"Hi." He kept his voice soft so as not to startle her.

"I wondered how long it would take you to get here."

"Wayne just called." She looked tired, and her face was pale. "How are you? Really."

"As well as can be expected."

"What's the plan?"

"Beats me." Her eyes welled up, but she squared her shoulders and held back the tears. "I can't even go home. It's not safe."

"I had an idea. Miss Tabitha has an empty room these days. I'm sure she'd be happy to have you stay with her until we catch this guy."

She groaned. "I can't afford to pay her and keep up my mortgage payments. That'll never work."

"I think she'd be happy to help you out, neighbor to neighbor." Anger seared up. "And if I have anything to say about it, this guy's days as a free man are few."

She shook her head. "I appreciate all you've done for me, and I understand your determination to solve the case, but you know as well as I do that this isn't the time for you to get involved in something outside your jurisdiction. Certainly not my case. People are starting to talk—"

"So I'm supposed to behave according to what gossips have to say." He had to exert almost superhuman effort to keep his temper under control. "Sorry. I don't work that way. I have a greater measuring stick, and I'd much rather answer to the One who gave it to me than to the chatterers."

Her cheeks colored. "Sorry. I'd just hate to think how my problems are affecting your reelection."

"Fine. So gossip is building, and there's a push to elect Ethan Rodgers on a write-in ballot, but I can't let circumstances change how I do things. I could never look myself in the mirror in the morning if I did that."

"I was afraid you'd say something like that."

"What did you want me to say? That I'd bail out on someone who needs help just to save my bacon? I don't work that way, Steph, and I think you know it."

She sighed. "I do."

"Now, how about you get into my car and we go talk to Miss Tabitha? And while I'm at it, maybe I should talk to Ethan. He's been renting one of her rooms for a couple of years now. He might give me some pointers on how to wrap up this case."

Steph caught her bottom lip between her teeth. The same urge he'd felt the night of the Fest hit Hal again. This time, his hand itched to gently tug her lip from where she'd caught it. But he couldn't. He didn't have the right. Even though he sure wished he did.

Once all this mess was cleared, and he knew where he stood with Steph, he would pursue it.

Now, though, he bent over in an exaggerated bow and added a flourish with his arm. "*Mademoiselle?* Your chariot awaits. Let's go see Miss Tabitha."

A chuckle burst from her. Hal promised himself to bring about as many repeats as possible—without turning himself into a clown. And then something else occurred to him. "You really shouldn't be alone at any time. I know this'll work well—staying with Miss Tabitha, I mean. But when you're not at her place or at the store…um…maybe we—you and I— can spend more time trying to figure out who's behind the siege. Together. You know. And that way you won't have to be alone. At all. For protection, of course."

Way to wow her, Benson. Smooth as sandpaper.

To his surprise, she nodded. "Makes sense. We have to solve this soon. And…I'm not really looking forward to facing this creep alone again."

He smiled, but at the same time, his conscience let off a warning twinge. Was he really being that self-serving? Was he working his way into her life only to explore the crush he'd had for so long? Or was he sincerely working to catch a thief? A drug dealer? A man capable of assaulting a defenseless woman?

Maybe it was equal parts of both. But was that honest? Was it ethical? How did it stack by God's measuring stick?

As he cranked up the car, he turned to his Heavenly Father. *Keep me honest, here, Lord. Don't let me get too carried away.*

Regardless, Hal intended to build a solid friendship with Steph. If nothing more developed, well, he'd deal with it at that point. In any case, it wouldn't hurt to have her in his life, even as a friend.

TEN

"Steph!" Miss Tabitha said. "What brings you here? I'm so glad to see you—oh, and you, too, Sheriff Hal."

From the twinkle in the older woman's green eyes, Steph knew she'd made a note of the two of them together once again. Before Miss Tabitha could decide to take a cue from the gossips in Loganton and spread the word, she gave her a hug. "We're here on business. Really."

Miss Tabitha planted her fists on her plump hips. "And what kind of business would bring you here of all places?"

Hal slipped inside the attractive foyer, closed the front door and stepped to Steph's side. She flashed him a grateful smile.

"Could we sit a bit, Miss Tabitha?" he asked.

"Oh, dear!" She shook her head. "I can't believe I forgot my manners. What's wrong with me today? Come on in to the parlor. Please."

In the parlor, Steph relaxed. She couldn't think back to when she'd last been able to really relax and feel at ease. Maybe Hal did have a point. Maybe she would be better off staying with Miss Tabitha than trying to go it alone at her place. At least, until the thief was caught.

She turned to their hostess. "You know the problems I've been having at the drugstore, right?"

The braided coronet of soft, white hair at the top of Miss Tabitha's head bobbed up and down. "Everyone knows about it."

"It just got worse."

Lively green eyes widened in horror. "Worse? How could it possibly have gotten any worse? A crazy criminal stealing drugs from your pharmacy and mugging you in that back alley's pretty rotten in my book."

"It got worse when he followed me home and slashed my tires."

"No!" Miss Tabitha looked truly distressed.

Steph stood and went to sit by her side. "I'm okay. Really. I am. But that brings me to the reason for our visit. Because my garage door was locked and he still got in…somehow, the sheriff doesn't think I should stay there alone—"

"Honey, you need to move in with me right this minute! Why, I have a nice ol' empty room upstairs with your name on it. And I won't hear a single bit of arguing on that, you hear?"

Steph chuckled. "I hear. In fact, Hal said you had a vacancy, and we wanted to see if you'd rent me the room—"

"Rent? At a time like this?" Miss Tabitha gave Steph's hand a little rap. "Don't you even bring it up again. What're neighbors for, Stephanie Lou Scott?"

For a moment, Steph missed her parents more sharply than she ever had before. But then Miss Tabitha took one of Steph's hands between hers, clasped it gently and smiled. "Honey, we're all given different gifts. The Good Lord blessed me with a real hunger to be hospitable, and how better could I ever honor Him than by welcoming a friend in need? Consider this your home."

A knot formed in her throat, and while Steph wanted to thank her kind friend, she found she couldn't get a single word out. Hal recognized her dilemma.

"You're wonderful, Miss Tabitha," he said. "And your beautiful home is the perfect place for Steph until we take care of this mess. There's always someone around here, isn't there?"

Footsteps in the foyer made all three turn. Ethan Rodgers and Tess Graver, his fiancée, had just arrived, their excitement palpable, their smiles radiant, the joy of their love contagious.

"Welcome home," Miss Tabitha called out. "What were you two up to this time?"

Tess turned to glance up at Ethan. "I actually got him to come with me when I stopped by the bakery. You won't believe how amazing that frosting tastes!"

"It's a good thing I won't have to wait long to taste it, then," Miss Tabitha answered. "Would you like to join us?"

"For a few minutes," Ethan answered. "We're supposed to get Killer back from the groomer. I say we leave him there and look forward to a peaceful, *quiet* future."

Tess gave her husband-to-be a gentle punch on the upper arm. "Give it up, will you? Our dog's name is Kiwi, and you're as crazy about the little guy as I am."

They sat close together on the love seat in front of the bay window. "I might be if he didn't freak every time he sees me."

Tess rolled her eyes. "What's up, Miss Tabitha?"

"Steph's moving into Joe's old room until Hal and the PD lock up that monster who's been terrorizing her."

Never let it be said that Miss Tabitha would beat around the bush. Steph gave the couple a wry smile. "He broke into my garage this morning and slashed my tires. By the time the PD got to the pharmacy, he'd looted the place—"

"He took everything?" Ethan asked, his eyes narrowed, his lean frame taut and ready to spring into action.

She wouldn't want to be on the wrong side of the law when this man was around. "All the controlled substances, schedule II, III, IV and Vs," Steph said. "Makes me wonder if the first time he was interrupted or afraid he'd run out of time."

"What exactly did he take that time?" the former agent asked.

Hal ran a finger around the rim of his hat where he'd plunked it on his knee. "Pseudoephedrine. Every bit Steph had in the place. She was keeping it all behind the counter, and he cleaned her out."

Ethan turned to Hal. "How about the additives?"

"He left the antifreeze and paint thinner behind the last time, but he took them today." Hal reached out a hand. "Hal Benson—pleased to finally meet you. I've heard a lot about you, and all of it good."

The men shook, Ethan returning Hal's long, steady stare. "Same here. I'm getting married on Friday evening, heading for our honeymoon on Saturday. Could I give you a hand until then?"

Steph saw Hal tighten his lips then take a deep breath. The gossips would have a field day when they heard the Chicago agent was on the case. They'd have more ammunition for the write-in campaign.

"We can use all the help we can get," Hal finally said.

Ethan gave a satisfied nod. "We'll have to go over every last piece of data you've gathered." He turned to Steph. "And I'll have questions for you, so you might want to write down everything, every last thing you remember, even how you felt at every incident. You never know what those impressions could reveal."

As Ethan spoke, something, a wisp of memory, teased Steph's thoughts. She reached for it, tried to grasp it, but it escaped. There was something...but she couldn't put a finger on it. And yet...maybe there was nothing. Maybe she just wanted there to be a clue they'd missed.

"I appreciate your help, but I don't want to distract you from all the preparations."

Tess laughed. "What preparations? All those hours I slaved over the details, he spent working out with his physical therapist. He'll forever thank you for keeping him too busy to have to think about flowers or candles or music—you get my drift."

Just then, a streak of black flew into the room, tore around the furniture, let out an exceptional yowl and then dashed out the archway to the dining room.

"What," Steph asked, "was that?"

"Why, Steph, my dear," Miss Tabitha said. "That's my darling little Bootsy. Isn't she something?"

Steph gulped. A look at Tess, another to Ethan and a final one at Hal did nothing to help. All four were fighting to keep from laughing.

Diplomacy, Steph. And tact. "Um…yeah. She's something."

"Come on." Miss Tabitha stood. "Let's go see the babies."

And she wants me to take home one of those beasties?

"Before you go," Tess said, laughter in her voice, "I'd like to ask you both to join us on Friday. The ceremony's at five forty-five, and the reception follows right after in the fellowship hall. And if you need a bribe to get you to say yes, Granny Annie, Uncle Gordon and Miss Tabitha will be doing the food."

Steph blushed. "Oh, no! You don't have to do that. I'm imposing enough by moving into Miss Tabitha's room. She won't even let me pay rent."

Tess reached for her fiancé's hand. "It'll be a blessing to have someone new in that room. Trust me on this."

Details from the drug bust came back to Steph's memory. The drug dealer Ethan and Tess brought to justice had rented one of Miss Tabitha's rooms. He'd also befriended Ethan. She wondered how the agent had dealt with the man's betrayal.

The engaged couple's laced fingers gave her the first clue. They'd turned to each other. Then, since she knew Ethan was close to Pastor Reams, she suspected he'd turned to that friend as well. If her presence in that vacant room helped erase unpleasant memories, she might just be able to make out a silver lining to her situation.

"Okay, then. I guess that's that," she said. "It'll be a pleasure to go to your wedding."

"Now how about Bootsy's babies, Steph?" Miss Tabitha asked. "You still have to choose yours."

This time, Steph refused to look at anyone else. She knew she'd either laugh or cry and didn't think that would be the right response to dear Miss Tabitha's efforts.

A feeling probably close to that of a sheep being led to the slaughter filled her. She stood and followed her hostess. "Let's go see Bootsy's babies."

The day after she moved into Miss Tabitha's lovely home, Steph received a not-so-lovely, but not unexpected, piece of mail. It came from the Bureau of Pharmacy Services and informed her she was the object of a formal investigation.

She'd had to inform the Bureau of the second robbery so as to remain in compliance with Bureau rules. They required licensed pharmacists to notify them of recurring losses of controlled substances. A second theft qualified. Besides, the authorities had notified the DEA of any drug theft, who, in turn, would have alerted the Bureau.

An investigation could result in the loss of her license. Even a suspension would be difficult to deal with. She was the only pharmacist in the area. In order for her to keep the pharmacy open and running, she would have to hire a substitute if they suspended her license.

The afternoon of the latest break-in, Steph had placed rush orders to her pharmaceutical suppliers, who'd gotten stock to her so she could open again quickly. Ever since then, she spent her hours working with a greater sense of appreciation. She looked at every nook and cranny of her store with more care; she relished every call for a refill, every customer who stopped by, every action she took, no matter how routine or seemingly unimportant.

And, in spite of the cost, she was glad she'd gone deep into her financial reserves and bought the upgraded surveillance system. While nothing could completely protect anyone, she felt a measure of reassurance now that it was in place.

On Wednesday, she helped Jimmy and Darcy prepare the store for the senior citizen invasion. By the time she handed Mr. Cutler his blood pressure meds, her spirits had improved, and she was able to laugh with one of her favorite customers.

"I hear tell you let Tabitha talk you into taking one of her feral beasties, sunshine," he said. "You'll be sorry!"

Although she'd felt something akin to that when she first laid eyes on Bootsy, the sweet little kittens had stolen her heart. "Aw, Mr. Cutler. They're just babies. And I'm going to take mine home. He won't ever be a wild, feral creature."

"Fine, fine, fine. If that's how you're going to be about it." He waggled a warning finger at her. "Let me tell you, though, even if it doesn't live out in a barn or the woods, it's the spawn of that Boots-thing of Tabitha's! That one'll scratch your eyes out if you let 'er get close."

Steph grinned. Bootsy did make a lasting impression. "She's lively, all right."

"Will you just quit your jawing already, Mason?" Miss Doolittle said. "Tabitha loves that cat, and the cat loves her. Why don't you try taking in a cat yourself? You might learn a thing or two."

Mr. Cutler's expression turned lofty. "I'll have you know, I'm allergic."

Miss Doolittle sniffed. "To picking up after anything— even yourself."

He glared. "How would you know?"

She smirked. "The cleaning ladies out at The Pines talk about your piles of books all over the place all the time…"

The rest of the seniors were just as much fun, if slightly less tart. After they headed out to hit Granny Annie's for their regular Wednesday-night supper, Steph and Jimmy closed up. As meticulous as she'd always been, now, with the specter of an investigation looming over her, Steph repeated her usual routine twice, just to make sure she hadn't forgotten anything.

Where she might have been tempted to follow the seniors to the diner just a week ago, these days Steph was enjoying the gourmet delicacies Miss Tabitha served her boarders. She and her "gentleman friend," Gordon Graver, Tess's great-uncle, ran a cooking school, and anyone who sat at Miss Tabitha's table benefited from the leftovers.

She especially appreciated not having to go to an empty home.

"Ready?" Hal asked when she locked the pharmacy door.

"You're like a well-timed homing pigeon," she said. "You're on time all the time, and my store seems to work like a magnet. But I must admit, I'm glad you're here. I…there's nothing pulling me home these days. The thought of someone who's out to hurt me, one way or another, is more than I can handle. And nights are nothing more than long hours where my imagination can do a number on me."

"That's too bad." He held the back door open for her. "When I stopped by that one night, it looked as though you'd taken a lot of care and used a lot of thought when you decorated your place."

"I did. But now he's ruined it for me." She sighed. "I do like the atmosphere at Miss Tabitha's. Even the nutty cat is fun."

They headed to the boarding house, and Hal stayed for supper, as he'd started doing since Steph moved in. After the meal, he and Ethan wandered off to Ethan's room, and Steph was sure they were going over every last piece of information about her case. While she was curious about the progress—or lack thereof—the authorities might be making, she'd chosen to play ostrich ever since the letter from the Bureau of Pharmacy Services arrived.

She'd thought a few times about that elusive sense of something she'd missed, something she couldn't remember. But no matter how hard she tried, she couldn't come up with anything at all. She wished she could.

Last night, Hal had come out from the law enforcement meeting of the minds, smiled and told her they were, of course, making progress. She'd smiled back, walked him out to the cruiser and not said another thing about the case.

Tonight, though, she refused to wimp out again. She was going to ask for details. So when the two men walked into the parlor, she stood and met Hal by the door. "Where does the investigation stand these days?"

He arched a brow. "You don't trust me?"

"That's not it at all. It's just that I'm the one whose business is on the verge of going under. I really think I should know what's going on."

"Tell you what. Trust me a little longer. Please."

Even though Steph knew she'd been spinning her wheels for a while, she again jumped at the chance to put off reality for another while. "Fine. But not for long. Who knows? Maybe I can help. They're targeting me, and I'm not dumb, you know."

The corners of his mouth twitched. "I would never dream of accusing you of that."

"Are you making fun of me?"

His laughter faded. "Not at all. I know how much you hated being questioned back when we were in school—you didn't like it when the teacher called you back from your daydreams, and the other kids sometimes called you names."

"Now you know that's what having ADD meant to me, even when I didn't have a name for it."

"But look how far you've come."

"Yeah. Far enough for some repulsive drug dealer to ruin all my efforts."

Hal placed both hands on her shoulders. "He won't. I won't let him. I'll take care of you."

Steph crossed her arms and placed a hand on each of his. "Oh, Hal. Don't do that. Don't make promises you don't know you can keep. I know you'll do your best to protect my store. But don't promise to take care of me—"

His eyes seemed to darken when he narrowed his gaze. "Trust me, Steph. This has nothing to do with the store, the thief or the drugs. It has everything to do with you. But I know right now is not the right time for this conversation. Once we've taken care of the other, we'll get back to it. I promise."

A shiver ran through her. Could he really be hinting at a…relationship? Romance? A future?

How did she feel about that?

But with Hal standing before her, in the middle of Miss

Tabitha's foyer, Steph knew he was right. This wasn't the time, not even to think about possibilities. She opened her lips to say good-night, but before she made a sound, he surprised her again.

"How about we take this slow and easy?" he said. "We can start with Ethan and Tess's wedding on Friday. They invited the two of us, and I'd love nothing more than to take you as my…" He took a deep breath. "As my date."

Steph caught her breath. The anticipation in his expression told her more than his offer had. How did she feel about a date with the sheriff?

A second ripple of… Oh, my! It was excitement and anticipation for her, too. "Yes. I *would* like that. I think we'll have fun."

Hal's sudden smile could have lit up the whole town. "Then Friday night it is." He took his hands from her shoulders, paused, then placed a finger on her cheek and, with the utmost care, smoothed it to her jaw, her chin. "Thanks."

Then he turned and left.

Steph propped her back on the door, stood there motionless, a tingling trail of warmth still on her skin. Imagine that. The very practical, down-to-earth sheriff had his own kind of magic in his touch.

He'd done it! He'd asked Steph Scott out for a date. But oh, man. Did he ever pick his time, or what? A wedding? For a first date? Talk about potential minefields.

The last thing Hal wanted was for Steph to think he was rushing her into a relationship or a commitment. Who cares if that's what he *really* wanted? He'd only grown to care more for her as he'd come to know her better. And there was infinitely more to like the more one came to know Steph Scott.

More to love…

She was kind, she was sweet, she was smart, hardworking, beautiful, she refused to hurt Miss Tabitha's feelings and she even laughed at his jokes. She also lived her faith; she had ever since he'd known her.

He knew she didn't expect him to perform phenomenal feats of investigative wizardry, but he also knew he wouldn't be able to live with his conscience if he didn't solve the rash of crimes that had run her from her home and threatened her store. He had e-mailed Ethan all the documents pertaining to her case, and the two men had pored over the details after dinner. Nothing much had jumped out at them.

"Looks like a pro's running this," Ethan had said. "No fingerprints, footprints, no hard evidence at all. All we have are a couple of vandalized boxes of merchandise, a picked backdoor lock, a ruined surveillance system and a trashed garage-door opener motor. Time to turn this investigation upside down."

"How?" Hal had asked.

"By looking for the users. Once we finger those, we can take the shortest path: follow the money. It'll always lead you where you have to go. Doesn't matter what kind of crime."

They'd agreed to work separately. Ethan would meet with Wayne and Maggie, who was his younger cousin, while Hal would go meet with the principal at the high school. He wanted to know if any student's grades had suddenly dropped or if any kid seemed suddenly flush with funds.

Tomorrow should prove to be an interesting day. He hoped it also turned out to be productive. He wanted Steph's troubles behind them. He wanted to see her laugh and smile without the shadow of fear holding her back.

He wanted to see where his feelings for her would ultimately lead.

* * *

Steph went shopping on Thursday evening after work. She found the most amazing forest-green dress that did wonderful things for her peachy-toned complexion and blond hair. The fabric, a soft, flowy knit, made her feel elegant and feminine, and she wished she could afford more pieces like it.

She hoped Hal liked the way she looked in the dress.

A pair of black peep-toe heels added height, which would never hurt, since her date—she could hardly believe she was going on a date!—was well over six feet tall. A light application of makeup enhanced her features, and her favorite lip gloss added the final touch.

When he arrived to pick her up on Friday, Hal stood in the doorway for a handful of seconds, according to him, stunned by her beauty. She wouldn't go so far as to call herself beautiful, but it was great to know her efforts had succeeded.

As had his. His navy suit fit him to perfection, and the light blue shirt, navy and burgundy tie and white handkerchief peeking in a triangle from the breast pocket lent him an air of perfect elegance.

Steph was as stunned as Hal.

They made pleasant conversation on their way to the church. She stole a dozen looks at Hal in the car, and when they arrived, she couldn't help the satisfaction of knowing they looked good together.

A crowd filled the sanctuary, and finding a spot for them in the pews proved no easy feat, but finally, they were seated as the organ thundered out an announcing chord. Silence reigned among the guests.

The sweet, familiar notes of Vivaldi's "Spring" filled the room instead of the more traditional "Bridal Chorus" from *Lohengrin.* A moment later, a gasp of pleasure rose from the congregation as Tess appeared on her great-uncle Gordon's arm. The bride's gaze was fixed on the altar, where her groom, accompanied by a handsome red-haired man in a wheelchair, awaited.

Ethan's features revealed his every emotion. From where she stood, Steph could actually see the sheen of moisture in his eyes, eyes that never left the radiant woman making her way up the aisle.

In fervent voices, Ethan and Tess spoke their vows before God and men.

Steph glanced sideways and met Hal's gaze. A shimmer of pleasure flew through her. In his expression she saw more than simple friendship. Maybe affection. Maybe more.

If she gave her imagination free rein, she'd say it might even be the stuff of dreams, the stuff of romance.

ELEVEN

All the noisy happiness of the reception couldn't dim the powerful impact of the moment Hal had shared with Steph when the bride and groom had spoken their vows. He'd then escorted his date from the sanctuary, down the receiving line and into the fellowship hall, where food and festivity awaited. He'd done it all in a haze of possibilities.

It encouraged him that Steph hadn't bolted from his side—his intense response to the ceremony hadn't been so over-the-top as to scare her away. Better yet, if he let wishful thinking take hold, he could almost convince himself he'd seen a similar response in her gaze. After all, she hadn't looked away.

Now they stood just inside the fellowship hall at the church, surrounded by the crush of guests, and Hal wondered how long it was going to take him to get through them all and reach the vast punch bowl.

"Would you like something to drink?" he asked Steph, raising his voice over the babble and the music.

"Love some!" She glanced toward the table where the beverage fountain reigned supreme. "But do you really think you're going to make it there in the next century?"

He winked. "Anything for milady!"

"You're nuts!"

"Maybe, but I'm also dying for something to drink. Want to come with me, or would you rather wait here?"

"I'll wait until they let us through to the tables. I'll see if they're using place cards. If they aren't, then I'll make sure to snag two chairs for us."

"Sounds like a plan. Be right back—with drinks!"

Even though he didn't want to leave her side, he needed some distance to get hold of his feelings. It had been intense. What had he been thinking? To ask Steph to come to the wedding as his guest?

Love made a man crazy, all right.

Had he pushed too far?

As Steph watched the guests pour in, she caught snippets of conversation. In a strange way, the crowd and their chatter all comforted her. She'd come back to open up her store in her hometown because she'd known she'd be welcomed and accepted here, and she could relate to the residents of Loganton. One of the toughest things about the events of the past few weeks was how they had changed her relationship with her fellow Logantonians.

Oh, the change was subtle; no one had snubbed her outright. But the glances and stares sent her way were getting old. She wanted the thief caught and her name cleared. She wanted to get back to doing what God had called her to do—to serve those who needed medication so they could continue to live out the Lord's plan for their lives.

At times, her anger threatened to overwhelm her. At other times, despair raised its nasty head. Whenever her emotions tried to take over, however, Steph reminded herself of her innocence, of the King she served, of the power of truth. She also remembered Hal's determination.

She had to trust.

"…Did you see them?" a woman asked behind Steph. "They're here together! Can you believe that?"

"If that's not a conflict of interest for 'im, then I sure don't know what is," another countered.

"You don't think she's…charming him into blindness about what she's done, do you?"

"Who knows? It's not as if she'd be the first woman who's tried to save herself by flirting with the man in charge of investigating her."

Steph drew in a sharp, rough breath. *Dear Lord Jesus! They're talking about me…us. Help us. Your will, Father God, Your will be done here, please.*

And then, anger, a righteous indignation, started a slow simmer. How dare they put themselves in the position of judge and jury? And at a wedding reception. This was supposed to be a joyous time. Instead, the gossips' mean-spirited words were tearing her and Hal down, and without basis. Such a nasty intrusion into a celebration.

What should she do? Should she turn around and defend herself and Hal? Or should she just walk away?

"And him wanting another turn in office," the first gossip added.

The second sniffed. "Thank goodness Ethan and Tess are settling in town after they get back from their honeymoon. I'm doing a write-in ballot. How about you?"

"Are you kidding me? When my choices are Hal the Hunky Romantic and Ed the Egomaniacal Flake? Whoever came up with the idea of a write-in ballot was using genius, pure genius…"

Miss Tabitha burst through a handful of bored-looking men not ten feet and three clots of women away from Steph. "Psst! Stephanie Lou! Over here."

Steph joined her landlady. "Wow! It seems as though the whole town's here tonight."

"Tess and Ethan wanted everyone to join them in celebrating their marriage. Don't they look sweet?"

"I wouldn't call them sweet. Romantic, blissful, deeply in love? Sure. But sweet? I don't think so. That's too wishy-washy."

"You understood what I meant." Then Miss Tabitha got that certain twinkle in her green eyes again. "And don't you and the sheriff make the loveliest couple!" She reached over and patted Steph's hand. "You've got more disappointed mamas glaring than I've seen in a long time."

Steph blushed.

"I did it!" Hal crowed, holding two punch cups high over his head as he skirted the clumps of women. "And I didn't even have to use my clout as a lawman to get 'em."

She blushed hotter. Had he heard what Miss Tabitha said? Steph sure hoped not. She also hoped he hadn't heard the gossips either. "Um…thanks."

Hal turned to the older woman. "Hey, there, Miss Tabitha. What's on the menu?"

"Oh, Annie's made a yummy squash bisque and the most wonderful ham. Wait until you taste the glaze she used. Mmm, good! And Gordon and I made buckets of hollandaise for the broccoli—it's too bad it's the wrong time of year for asparagus."

Steph's mouth watered. "That sounds wonderful. When do we eat?"

Miss Tabitha glanced over her shoulder toward the commercial kitchen the church had put in two years earlier. "As soon as Annie gets through the crowd to let Tess know. And look at that! She's not even heading toward the bride and groom yet. She's coming this way instead."

As her landlady shook her head, Steph watched Granny Annie wend her way around the many groups of guests who took the time to greet her. "She really does know everyone, doesn't she?"

Hal laughed. "Hey, I'm no dummy. That's the reason I want her on my side in the race."

Something in the vicinity of Steph's heart squeezed. He couldn't lose. He simply couldn't. "Do you think she's been 'politicking'—like she calls it—here?"

"She's talking everyone's ear off," Hal said with a smile. "I sure hope some of what she's saying is about my experience, dedication and how much I love my job."

Jimmy Miller walked up, an hors d'oeuvre-laden tray in his hands. "Hey, there, Miss Steph. Sheriff Benson. The food's awesome. You gotta try these…these triangle things with the cheese and green stuff inside. Wow!"

Steph took a golden pastry. "They're called spanakopita, Jimmy. They're one of Miss Tabitha's specialties, and totally delicious."

Miss Tabitha blushed as she picked up a crispy triangle. "I'm glad you like them. It's one of my favorite recipes. I just hope Gordon and I made enough."

Hal helped himself as well, and they all munched in delighted silence.

"Phew!" Granny Annie said when she finally broke through to them. "Looks like the line to get in is done." She pointed out the window just a few feet beyond Steph. "It's about time, too. This ain't a three-for-one sale down to the Shop For Less, you know. We been watching the line from the kitchen, wondering if we have anywhere near enough to feed this mob. Looks like everyone's here now, though, and we can finally get on with the show."

"If the diner's anything to go by," Steph said, smiling, "then the leftovers should be impressive. You always serve big and have enough to offer do-overs the next day."

The diner owner shrugged. "I always say, cook once, feed 'em twice—"

Crash!

Glass shattered behind Steph. Something whizzed past her. Another one. Yet a third. Then Granny moaned, and right before Steph's eyes, crumpled to the ground, a hideous red bloom spreading across her chest.

"Everybody down!" Hal yelled, whipping out his weapon. "Now!"

Steph didn't need another command, but once on her belly, she worked her way over to the motionless Granny, praying for her, pleading with God.

"Steph!" Hal called on his way to the door. "Call the PD. Have them call my office. Ask the dispatcher to send everyone they can get."

She did as he asked, impressed by how little time the dispatcher took to relay the urgent need.

After she hung up, all Steph knew was fear, anguish and misery. She heard the random bits and pieces of whispers from those around her. Most of the guests assumed the bullets had been meant for Ethan, since he'd recently taken down that drug dealer. But Steph knew better. The former agent could have been taken out more easily any number of times that evening—as he and his bride walked out of the church, as they stood outside shaking hands with their guests or as they walked to the fellowship building.

The bullet that hit Granny had been meant for Steph.

Oh, some might say she was getting paranoid. But who could blame her? She felt as if she was wearing a target on her back. And she had been repeatedly attacked. The question was, of course, why?

She had no idea.

She also didn't know whether it had been meant as a warning or whether it was to have finished her off.

In either case, she prayed it wouldn't finish off innocent, uninvolved Granny Annie. She took the older woman's pulse and noted how labored her breath had become.

If the world around Steph were to have started to melt like a timepiece in a Salvador Dalí painting, it wouldn't have surprised her. Nothing felt real. Her earlier anger returned.

Wrong, wrong, wrong. This was all wrong—sick, horrifying. It was supposed to be a wedding, a celebration of love, not the murder of a dear, sweet older lady.

Steph held on to Granny's hand, kept track of her pulse, willing the sassy senior to hang in there, to fight on. Although weak, the heartbeat remained steady.

Miss Tabitha joined her and took off Granny's formerly immaculate apron. With quick, spare motions, she folded the cotton fabric, hiding the original stain and hole, and then pressed the pad she'd made against the fallen woman's chest, applying pressure to the shocking, spreading blood.

Steph couldn't have said how long it took, but eventually sirens blared closer. What seemed like an army of cops burst into the hall, followed by three EMTs. When the two men and one woman converged on Granny, she sat back; her body suddenly felt boneless. She couldn't stand, couldn't do more than feel the agony of watching someone she loved suffer and creep closer to death.

Shivering, and numb but for the ache in her heart, Steph offered fragmented prayers, feeling more alone than ever. She wished she had someone to turn to right then. Hal. Not as the sheriff or a law enforcement officer, but as the solid, steady man she knew, the man she'd come to trust. She felt anything but steady right then. At a time like this, when a wonderful woman could lose her life, Steph craved the reassurance his company gave her.

What if Granny Annie lost her life? How would Steph ever reconcile that loss with the knowledge it had come about because of her?

Facing that loss alone would be a very, very hard thing to do.

The intrusion of the gossip at the reception had angered Steph. But it hadn't been the only intruder on the festivities. A more ominous intruder had also crashed the party. The gunshots had burst in, sending a message Steph couldn't mistake.

The shooter was after her. Just like the rock thrower had been.

Again, the question was why?

He'd already cleaned out the pharmacy of all drugs. What did he have against her? She hadn't struck out at him; he'd come after her everywhere she went: at her store, in the alley, at her home, in her car and now at the wedding of mere acquaintances. No matter how she looked at her situation, she kept coming back to that one irritating question.

Why?

"That's the key," Hal said, "isn't it?"

Only when he responded did Steph realize she'd voiced the question out loud. "I really don't get it. From where I'm sitting, he's gotten everything he's wanted. Why would he continue to come after me? I don't have anything he wants—nothing!"

Instead of agreeing with her, as she'd expected, Hal settled more comfortably into his waiting-room armchair. "I'm sure you do—or at least, I'm sure he thinks you do. I'm also sure we've missed something. But since we've missed it, we're in the dark."

Steph couldn't relax; she felt awful. "And that's why a wedding was ruined and the dearest woman is…is…"

She waved toward the double doors to the O.R. The words wouldn't take form; she couldn't bring herself to put her greatest fear into words.

All she'd ever wanted was to help people, and in the end, all she'd done was hurt them. Well, she wasn't so totally off-kilter as to think she was the guilty party in all this, but she was the pharmacy owner, and she hadn't been able to keep a thief out of the drugs. While she supposed any other pharmacist who'd come and set up shop in Loganton would have fared the same, it was still her store that had drawn the criminal.

"Don't blame yourself. It's not your fault."

Hal's softly spoken words cut through her painful thoughts. "How'd you know what I was thinking?"

"I'm a cop. We know how to beat ourselves up better than just about anyone else."

"There must be something I could have done better. Maybe if I'd had the money to get more—better, to get better locks. Maybe if I'd been able to afford the surveillance cameras sooner…"

"Like I said, don't. It won't do you or Granny any good." He reached out and, with an exquisite gentleness, took her hand in his. "What happened when you installed that very expensive, very powerful system?"

Steph heard a siren approach, an ambulance…another emergency. She shuddered then turned back to Hal. "Sure. But if I'd had it to begin with, we might have caught his picture at the time of the first break-in."

"And what makes you think he wouldn't have disabled it then?"

"Would he have known I had a system from the start?"

"Of course. He had to have scoped out the store before he mugged you the first time. He knew where to wait for you when you were leaving. The lack of clues tells me he's a pro. You're not his first victim. His kind doesn't just hit up any random store out of the blue. He does his homework—"

The door from the E.R. receiving bay burst open. A nurse led the way, running, concentration on her every feature. Two EMTs pushed a gurney between them, running as well.

With a firm punch, the nurse hit the automatic door open button on the wall. The E.R. doors, opposite the O.R. doors, swung open. As the EMTs rolled the gurney to the door, the nurse went in, calling, "Teen gunshot—and possible overdose. Stat!"

Steph sucked in a harsh breath. She stretched to catch a glimpse of the patient, wondering which one among all the kids she'd spoken to she'd failed to reach with her message. And then, at the sight of the familiar face…

"No!" she cried, stood, took steps toward the victim. "No, no, no!"

Hal caught her in his strong arms. "Easy, easy."

She struggled, desperate to free herself. "Don't you understand? I have to go, I have to help him—it's Jimmy!"

With what strength she had left, she fought him, but Hal's size would have won even on a good day. And today was the worst she'd ever known. Steph felt as though she couldn't catch a breath, as though the walls were crushing in on her, as though every time she turned around, another mugger was beating on her back.

A sob tore through her, and she realized tears had been pouring down her cheeks. The flow continued. The sobs multiplied. Through it all, Hal held her, cradled her head in one of his large hands, held her shaking, sobbing body against his sturdy, solid frame.

She couldn't have said how long they stood like that. At some point, however, Hal's warmth penetrated the icy fear that had overtaken her. She heard his steady heartbeat as he held her head against his chest. She caught the light scent of something woodsy and clean and realized she could identify the fragrance as uniquely his.

She trusted this man. She could depend on him. And not just in this time of turmoil. Hal Benson was the kind of man any woman would be blessed to have at her side. A sudden need to keep him there, with her, close and comforting, swept over her. How had this happened? When had she come to care so much for a man who, only a few weeks earlier, had been a virtual stranger?

Trouble made for odd connections.

Lifting her head, she looked up into Hal's face. The concern and care she saw in his expression eased something in her. He understood. He might not know Jimmy as well as she did, but he understood her frustration and her anguish. He'd agreed to work with her in her campaign to keep drugs out of the school.

But they'd failed.

Or at least they'd failed Jimmy.

Now Steph had two loved ones behind those frightening doors.

"Thanks," she told Hal.

"I wouldn't leave you."

"I'm glad. As it is—" she wiped tears off her cheek "—I don't know how I'm going to make it without losing my mind. And they don't deserve a basket case waiting out here. Especially Jimmy. He's going to need a lot of help."

If he makes it.

Neither said it, but the thought, the awful possibility, hung between them. To clear her head, Steph asked the question burning through her thoughts. "Do you think he stole the pseudoephedrine?"

"He could have, I'm sorry to say."

"He certainly had the opportunity. And he had the opportunity to tamper with all the merchandise."

"How about the first night? The mugging. Do you think he might have been the one? Think. Think hard."

She thought back, going over every second of that horrible time. For a moment, that fleeting idea…that elusive something hovered in her memory, but it remained out of reach. And nearly drove her mad with her inability to put a finger on it, to say just what it might be.

"Unfortunately," she said, "I think he could have. I'd sent him home because the storm was about to hit. I was alone closing up, so he could have grabbed his disguise—which wasn't more than a hoodie over a ski mask, from what I could see—and waited for me to walk out."

Hal's slow nod brought his sandpapery chin against her forehead. The slight friction felt good, real, honest and very much *there.* Everything else in her life had turned into one of the Salvador Dalí paintings that had oozed into her thoughts back at the fellowship hall. She now understood, with a visceral knowledge, the true meaning of the word *surreal.*

Another thought followed on the heels of her trip down eccentric-artist lane. "The nurse said gunshot wound. Do you think he was the shooter at the reception, and then one of your people shot him?"

"Don't you remember? He was standing next to Granny—
to us—when the shooter struck. Besides, my guys would have
followed him here if they'd been the ones to hit him."

Resignation settled on Steph. "Then there's only one ex-
planation. He's doing drugs, and he got on the wrong side of
a dealer even back at the reception."

"I'm afraid that's about the way I read it, too."

So the shot hadn't been for her. Poor Jimmy. What a
tragedy of bad choice. She was thankful Hal still had an arm
around her. She didn't know if she could have held herself
upright on her own. Grief drained her, left her weak and
feeling vulnerable. Jimmy shouldn't be behind those doors,
fighting for his life. He was only sixteen. He should be home
sleeping, healthy and looking forward to a wonderful, productive future.

Instead, today might be his last day. Deep sadness filled
Steph. She knew he didn't have much of a relationship with
God. They'd talked a couple of times about faith, and the need
for the Father, but he'd never moved much beyond asking
about her beliefs.

*Please, Lord, if it's Your will, let him live. I want another
chance to show him how much better, how much richer, life
is when one lives it by Your Word. Don't let him die like this…*

She eased a few inches from Hal and met his gaze. "Do
you think he'll make it?"

"Who?" asked Karla, Granny Annie's youngest niece, as she
walked into the waiting room. "Did someone else get shot?"

Steph and Hal traded looks. He shrugged. She turned to the
girl. "Jimmy Miller was just brought in by ambulance. It
seems he, too, was shot."

Karla shook her head. "He's been really weird lately. I'd
wondered…"

Steph waited for the girl to continue, but when Karla didn't, she said, "You'd wondered?"

"I'd wondered if he'd started using."

Karla looked tired and drained, and Steph's heart ached for her. She and Granny were inseparable. What a mess… what a night.

"Is Jimmy the only one who's started to turn 'weird' at school?" Hal asked.

Karla shook her head. "It's been growing. I hate it, but we're seeing more stoners all the time."

Just then, Dan McGreevy, the high-school principal, ran into the waiting room. "I got a call. Jimmy Miller was shot behind the school. How is he? Have you seen him?"

Hal held out a hand, and the two men shook. "I don't know how he's doing. They just rushed him in about ten minutes ago."

Dan ran a hand through his dark hair, leaving it rumpled, his forehead lined with worry, stress evident in every line of his body. "I just don't get why they do this to themselves. But this…a shooting! We've never had anything like this happen at Loganton High before."

They all fell silent, each clearly busy with private thoughts. Then the principal stuck his hands in his pockets.

"All right, then." He pinned Steph and Hal with a steely stare. "It's not going to do any good for me to just moan and groan. So what are we going to do about it? How are we going to keep from having another Jimmy go down?"

TWELVE

Hal, Steph and Dan McGreevy agreed to meet on Wednesday evening to devise a plan of action. All three knew the situation couldn't go on as it was, growing worse with time.

Since he knew she wouldn't leave, Hal stayed with Steph at the hospital until the surgeon came through the O.R. doors. The young physician walked up to them, removing her sterile hairnet as she approached. "You're waiting to hear about Mrs. Griswold, right?"

Karla stepped up. "I'm her niece. How is she?"

"It wasn't easy, but we found the bullet, cleaned the wound, sutured all we could and now it's a matter of wait-and-see. She's no youngster, but she's also not nearly as old as she looks or acts. I'm hoping that and her excellent health will help her pull through."

"Prayer," Steph whispered.

"Can't hurt," Dr. Bailey said. "But the three of you need more than prayer right now. You need to get some sleep, otherwise you won't be any help to her."

Steph nodded but didn't budge. Then she squared her shoulders and looked up at the doctor. "Before I leave, I have to know how Jimmy Miller's doing, too. He works for me and was brought in a little while ago with a gunshot wound and a possible overdose."

Dr. Bailey held up a hand. "Hang on. I'll get someone from the E.R. to come and update you—if they can. Do you know anything about a family?"

"I haven't seen anyone," Steph said. "But if they came, they must have been taken straight to him. I don't think this is the only entrance to the E.R., right?"

"No, this waiting room is near the ambulance entrance. His parents would have come in through the hospital main doors. You wouldn't have seen them from here. Let me go check on what I can do."

Ten minutes later, a nurse walked out of the E.R. She walked up to them, her expression serious. "You're waiting to hear about James Miller, right?"

Hal stepped forward. "I'm Sheriff Benson, and this is Jimmy's employer, Stephanie Scott."

"They stopped the bleeding, stabilized him and are sending him up to the ICU."

Hal kept his gaze on Steph, who swallowed hard, then covered her mouth with a shaky hand. "Is he…will he make it?"

The nurse's expression remained serious if neutral. "I'm afraid that's all I can tell you. You might want to contact his parents in the morning. I'm sure they'll update you then."

Although Steph looked to Hal as though she wanted to ask more questions, she only gave the nurse a tight smile then turned to him. "I'll be back here in a couple of hours. I won't bother opening the store. I don't think anyone will have a problem with that once they know what happened to Jimmy."

"You need more than a couple of hours' sleep," he said. Then, turning to Karla, who'd remained silent, he added, "You, too. Let's all be smart about it, get enough rest so we're good for something and meet back here at…oh, let's say noon."

The two women agreed, reluctantly, but they did agree. Hal walked them to their vehicles, and then, because he knew she was wearing a figurative bull's-eye on her back, he followed Steph to the rooming house. Only after he saw her close the door with its large, oval glass insert did he head on home. Pepper was not going to be too happy with him. At least he'd stopped by on his way to the hospital to let her out.

He'd reached the point where he almost dreaded sleep. He didn't want to see what the morning would bring. He suspected whatever else it might be, it certainly wouldn't be good for Steph.

They had found no clues, no evidence, on the church grounds.

The next day, Steph left the hospital with pitifully little more to go on than what she'd had when she arrived. The Millers had been kind enough to tear themselves away from their critically ill son, which hadn't been her intention at all, and had come to thank her for her care and concern. The evidence of their shock and distress was etched on their faces and clear in the way they moved. It seemed to Steph as though they felt they carried an unbearable weight on their shoulders.

If their son survived, he might then be charged.

What a nightmare.

Drugs. They'd been developed to ease mankind's suffering. How—*why?*—the wonder of their use had been perverted to destroy escaped her. She only knew they'd become a means for human greed to grow unchecked.

After she left the hospital, Steph drove to the store in a haze of something that felt close to despair. Why she'd decided to go there, she wasn't sure. She couldn't open up for business, not after she'd left the CLOSED sign out all morning long. Besides, she hadn't made arrangements for anyone to come and help her…a substitute for Jimmy. It just didn't feel right.

But she couldn't stay away either. Maybe she just needed another opportunity to run her hand over the counter where she'd handed out so many life-giving medications. Or maybe she needed to walk the aisles she'd filled with everyday necessities. Or maybe it would be enough to just stand in the store and appreciate what she'd built from nothing more than a dream.

It hurt to think that dream might come to a rude end through no fault of her own.

When she unlocked the back door, she stepped in, and then threw the lock again. She didn't want any surprise visitors—of the dangerous kind, of course. Moments later, the phone began to ring.

Out of years of habit, she ran in past the damaged—for a second time now—pharmacy door to yank the receiver and answer. "Hello—er…Scott's Pharmacy. How can I help you?"

As she listened to the official on the other end, her stomach knotted, chills ran through her and her world tilted on its axis in a way she feared she might never right again. She only managed to respond with a handful of murmurs; no more was expected of her. Her fate had been decided. At least for the moment. And there was nothing more she could do. Not right now.

"I understand." She hung up.

The nightmare continued. Her license had been suspended pending the conclusion of the investigation. If she wanted to continue doing business, she would have to hire a replacement. For her.

But how was she going to pay someone else? She still had to pay the rent, utilities, product costs and, while she didn't lead an extravagant lifestyle, she still needed something to live on. She'd been getting along before, but not with any great margin, certainly not for this kind of expense. A licensed pharmacist didn't come cheap—she knew!

"Lord…You say You don't give us more to deal with than You equip us to handle. I've always believed this, but now? Now this really feels like too much. And I don't know that You're the one who's actually given me this."

The silence in the store threatened to overwhelm her. If she stayed much longer, she could wind up on the road to depression. That wouldn't help anything. And it wasn't the kind of attitude God really expected of her.

Even though the thought of all expectation was more than she felt she could handle right then.

She grabbed her purse and keys, and with a tissue in one hand to dry up the random tear she knew would fall, she went out the back door. In the alley, on her way to the car, she began to compose the ad she would have to place in the Charlotte and Raleigh newspapers. And she decided to stop by the flower shop and pick up a couple of arrangements before she returned to the hospital to check on Granny and Jimmy.

As bad as things had gone for her, they were far worse for the two of them. She should never forget that.

That, and her knowledge of God's mercy and goodness.

She had to hold fast to her faith.

A week and a half later, Steph had interviewed four pharmacists, spent more hours at the hospital than she cared to count, prayed what felt like hours' worth of prayers and planned a more structured aggressive approach to her drug-prevention program with Dan and Hal.

Granny Annie was well on her way to recovery, and while Jimmy would survive, he had a long way to go before he could leave the hospital. Meth had its claws well into him, and his parents were working with the physicians to put him on the road to detox. Steph again marveled at the way the potent poison better known as methamphetamine worked. Jimmy had only been using the drug for a couple of months. Even so, withdrawal was proving as great a challenge as the gunshot wound.

Once he won those two battles, Jimmy would have to face the juvenile justice system. And school…well, catching up wouldn't be easy. He would have to repeat his junior year. Steph hoped he did, rather than just drop out. And that he then went on to at least graduate if not pursue college as well.

Jared Hardy, Steph's temporary pharmacist, was scheduled to start Monday and came with an impressive background and great references—she'd checked them all. He'd worked for a number of large chain stores, and his bosses raved about his meticulous attention to detail. His vast knowledge of pharmacology and professional manner had impressed her when she'd interviewed him. The last thing she could afford was to hire someone who'd falsified or even embellished his background.

She'd decided to go on, not to surrender. Watching Jimmy and Granny fight for their lives had made her even more determined to persevere than ever before. She wouldn't let a criminal ruin everything she'd worked for. Somehow, she had to believe God would provide a way for her pharmacy to survive.

The Lord she loved and served would help her and Hal catch the creep who'd done this to Granny, Jimmy and, yes, to her as well.

But by the time Jared had manned the pharmacy counter for three hours, Steph had yet another battle to fight, this one against worry. Jared seemed stiff and uncomfortable dealing with the customers. He did know his pharmacology up one side and down the other, but there was more to a successful small-town pharmacist than counting pills or compounding formulas.

Her regulars commented as they left.

She reminded them he was a newcomer and needed time to get comfortable with them. Or so she hoped.

How was she going to approach her replacement and discuss the situation? Especially since he didn't seem to realize what was happening. Besides, Jared was about twenty years older, and her upbringing and manners had left her with a distinct bias toward respecting and honoring her elders. She didn't want to offend the man.

Oh, get a grip, Steph! Manners? She was thinking about *manners* when she had to deal with an employee's workplace problem? One he clearly didn't realize he had?

But Jared did have a problem. And it was serious.

Darcy walked in. "Hey there, business mogul! How's it going now that you're a real employer?"

Steph grabbed her friend by the elbow and dragged her back outside. "Oh, Darce, you have no idea. I don't know what to do about my new pharmacist. At this rate, he's going to sink my business in one day's time."

"What do you mean? Didn't you make sure he knew what he was doing before you hired him?"

Steph sent him a glance through the wide plate-glass window. "No, no, it's not that. He's great with the meds—and I checked every one of his references all the way back in his career. It's just in the other part of the job that he's lacking. He's not good with the customers."

Darcy peered at Jared, concern on her freckled face. "How so?"

"Oh, you know. People like to feel they're more than a number. You have to talk to them, let them know you care. But he's so serious, and I don't think he knows how to make small talk. You know how Logantonians are. Everyone knows everyone here, and they do like to chat."

"Maybe he thinks he has to remain detached to be a good professional. You know, like a doctor or a lawyer. Or maybe it's because he's new here. Give him some time. He'll probably relax after a few days, and then you'll wonder what you got all in a twist about."

"But what if by then Scott's is history?"

"Then why don't you talk to him? You're the boss, you know." The pop of a bubble accented Darcy's words.

"I can't afford to offend him. He might quit on me, and I need him here." The memory of her last, sad ATM machine receipt danced in her head. "I've lost more business than I care to think about since the night I was mugged. I can't shut down again and start hunting for another replacement. Besides, I don't know that I can make myself fire anyone."

"Fire him? Steph! You're getting way ahead of yourself. All you have to do is tell him what you expect. Tell him to ask folks about their kids and grandkids. It's the easiest way to break in to the Loganton scene—if there is such a thing."

"It would still be a scolding."

"So give him a *gentle* scolding."

Steph clasped her hands and slanted Jared a glance. "I don't think I can do that—I know, I know. Wimpy."

"So you can't talk to him, but you can let him ruin your store."

"No…but—"

"What do you mean, but? Come on, Steph. If it comes down to it, and he really doesn't work out, you're going to just have to get tough and fire the guy. So before it gets to that, do what you have to do. You've worked too hard to let a grump tear it all down. Tell him to take a charm pill and get over himself."

As Steph wavered, Darcy pressed her point. "I know you don't want to have a nasty confrontation on your new employee's first day, but you know that old song 'You Can't Always Get What You Want.'"

Steph rolled her eyes and shook her head.

"No, really." Darcy laid her hand on Steph's shoulders. "Look at me. Do you really think all I ever wanted to do is clean Miss Tabitha's house and your store?"

When Steph cringed, Darcy hurried to say, "Oh, don't get me wrong. I appreciate everything everyone does to help, but I've had dreams, too."

Steph winced. Others had it much worse than she did. "I'm so sorry—"

"Don't be. That's just life. You do what you have to do to survive. Now, if *you* want your store to survive, you're going to have to do something about your grump."

"He's not really a grump. He's just no Miss Personality— well, Mr. Personality. But you do have a point. I can't just let it go on."

She looked inside again, and, from the expression on Mr. Cooper's face as he waited for his meds, she figured she'd been gone long enough. She turned back to Darcy. "Did you come by because you needed something?"

"Nah. Just popped in to see how things were going." The worry Steph now realized Darcy had hidden lined her friend's forehead. "I know it's been tough for you, and I…I feel really, really bad about all of it."

"Oh, Darce…" She hugged her friend. "Thanks. Now scoot. I have work to do. And I'm sure Miss Tabitha has plenty for you, too."

Steph watched her friend hurry down the street then took a deep breath and walked back into the store. Sounds of a disagreement reached her before she reached the pharmacy counter. Chad Adams had just arrived with the day's delivery and wanted to put the cases where he always did. Jared had other ideas.

"I really can't let an unauthorized person in this part of the pharmacy." Steph's substitute looked ready to dig in his heels. "I don't know who you are. Please leave the boxes in the store-room, and one of us will take care of them later."

Chad dropped the boxes just outside of the pharmacy door. A frown lined his brow. "I might not be a pharmacist, but I'm sure qualified to put stuff where it makes sense. And from where I'm standing, it sure ain't back in no store-room. Anyone walking in the store could get at it without you seeing."

Jared frowned. "In my experience, deliveries have always been left in the storeroom. I'll make sure no one has access to the room."

Chad shoved his hands in his pockets. "Where's Steph? She knows what she's doing *and* what I'm doing."

Steph stepped forward to bring the confrontation to an end, but then it occurred to her it might be best if the two men resolved their differences on their own. They were going to have to get along day after day. She made herself wait and see what would happen.

Jared shook his head. "The store's had a problem with break-ins and drug theft. I can't run the risk of more drugs dis-appearing. I might wind up behind bars or without a license."

Chad waved at the pharmacy counter. "No one broke in while Steph was standing behind that window there. Besides, there ain't no place a person can't break into who really wants to and has half a brain."

When Jared didn't budge, Chad went on. "Look, let's just

get on with this delivery. I want my licorice, and then I gotta get a move on."

Jared blinked. "Licorice?"

Anyone would've thought Chad had suggested intergalactic travel. Time to ditch her case of wimpiness.

"Okay, gentlemen." Steph stepped out from behind her concealing shelves and dropped a two-pound bag of candy on the pharmacy counter. "Here, Chad. It's on the house, and please excuse Jared. He's new, and we haven't had the time to go over all our systems yet. Just put the boxes where you always do."

Jared clamped down on his lips until they became a thin white line then gave her a sharp nod, turned and went to work on a called-in prescription. Chad headed out to the truck, licorice rope in the corner of his mouth.

Steph counted the seconds until Chad slammed the back door to continue his rounds. Then, quaking inside but bolstered by a quick prayer and Darcy's encouragement, she stepped behind the pharmacy counter.

"I'm sorry, Jared. I wasn't as thorough as I should have been about my routines here, so we do need to go over a few things." His look wasn't full of sweetness and light, but Steph had to go on. "I understand and appreciate your concern for your license. Believe me. I have hated every second since mine was suspended. And Chad is right. If you want to check with the authorities, you'll see the break-ins didn't happen because of my negligence or carelessness."

Doubt crossed his face. "The Bureau wouldn't have suspended your license without good reason, would they? A suspension is a drastic step."

"It's drastic, but when controlled substances were stolen for a second time, they pretty much had no choice. They had to start the investigation, and as crazy as it makes me to say so, I would have done the same thing had I been in their position."

Wonder of wonders, she really meant every word she said.

Jared glanced at the back door. "Don't you think that delivery man checked out the layout back here the first day he showed up? Did you ever think he might be the one who helped himself to the drugs?"

To her dismay, Steph realized the thought had never crossed her mind. "I'm sure the authorities have vetted him. They've known our system from the start."

But had they looked at Chad? Hal had never mentioned it. How could she have missed such a glaring possibility? Had she been so busy thinking about the impact the spate of crimes was having on her that she hadn't given basic logic enough consideration?

Jared shrugged. "Fine, Miss Scott. We'll do things your way. But I don't feel comfortable letting anyone behind the counter."

"I understand."

Maybe he'd done her a favor in spite of his stiff demeanor. He'd pointed her in a new direction. As she walked from the pharmacy to the cosmetics aisle, she felt as though a weight only slightly lighter than the one she'd seen on Jimmy's parents settled on her shoulders. How many people had been harmed by the stolen drugs?

She'd never felt so low.

She'd failed. She hadn't even had the presence of mind to consider something so obvious that even a newcomer to town had picked up on right away.

"Father, help me," she whispered then pulled out her cell phone. At the rate she was going, she had to add a couple of numbers to her speed dial list. After two rings, a familiar voice answered.

"Hello."

"Hal? It's Steph. I have a couple of questions for you…"

THIRTEEN

Every inch of her body felt tight enough to snap. She suspected her eyes were flashing the proverbial flames of rage, and the top of her head felt as though it might blow off.

"What else have you kept from me?" Steph asked Hal. "Here I thought we'd agreed to work together. Do you even know what together means?"

When she'd called Hal after her confrontation with Jared, he'd told her he'd meet her at the store as she closed up for the night. Curiosity had sizzled all day, and when he'd finally showed up, she'd thought they'd make progress…somehow. Instead, he'd stunned her.

Not only had the Loganton PD investigated Chad Adams right after the mugging but they'd also known he'd lost his last job in Winston-Salem because he'd been busted for possession of marijuana while on the job. And what kind of work had he done? He'd been a security guard.

They'd even had him under surveillance the whole time. No one had bothered to tell her.

She glared at the sheriff. "It never occurred to you I had the right to know the deliveryman, the person who walked into my pharmacy every single day, was a drug user?"

"As it often happens during an investigation, we decided

it would be best to hold some information back until the appropriate time."

She scoffed. "Even I watch TV, Sheriff Benson. I know you law enforcement types only do that to trip up the criminal. Were you trying to trip me up? Did you think I'd plotted the whole thing with Chad?"

His cheekbones reddened. "No, I did not think you'd planned the whole thing with Chad Adams. I'm not that stupid."

Crossing her arms, she gave him a glare. "But Wayne Donnelly and Maggie Lowe are. Is that what you're saying?"

"I have said nothing of the kind."

"But you're also not denying it. Which tells me they still think I'm involved."

He had the grace to look uncomfortable. "They're just covering all the bases—like good cops should."

Steph fought the urge to roll her eyes like Darcy did. "Let's just get beyond this, okay? So then, what else have you not told me?"

Hal tried—tried—to look nonchalant. He didn't pull it off. "I don't know if we updated you on what we learned from Jimmy."

This time, Steph didn't hold back. She did what felt like a very Darcy-like eye roll. "Of course, you didn't update me on what you learned from Jimmy. What do you know?"

"Well, the doctors didn't let us question him until recently, you know. So I haven't delayed *that* much. He'd been buying meth from another kid at school—we've spoken to that boy, and he's been charged with dealing drugs." Hal ran a hand through his brown hair, leaving it rumpled, which made him look more approachable, less official. "You know Jimmy doesn't have much money. He started using, and soon enough he wanted more meth. More meth means he needed more money. The seller got Jimmy to sell at school in payment for his own stash."

"And…?"

"And their boss made them throw that rock at you. Obviously, he saw you as a threat. He thought you knew something that would hurt his business. But that's when Jimmy had enough. After the rock incident, he just wanted out." With what seemed like admiration, Hal shook his head. "He actually told the supplier to leave Loganton or he'd go to the PD with what he knew—as little as it seems to be. It looks to me like the bullet that hit Granny was meant for him."

"Oh, no!" Tears welled up. "That poor kid. He must be feeling awful about Granny, and that's on top of his own troubles. What else did he tell you?"

"That's it. Neither one of the boys is willing to say much more. They did say the man pulling the strings isn't local. They don't know him, since he hangs out in the dark, but they're scared. Whoever this guy might be has the kind of grip on them we can't begin to break."

"They're willing to die to protect his identity?"

"How do you figure?"

"Do you think the mastermind doesn't know the boys are in your experienced hands? You don't think he's figured out they'll talk sooner or later?"

"Not if he's played his cards right. Both kids have an addiction to deal with. So even if they do clean up, recidivism rates are through the roof. He figures all he has to do is get them using again, and since he's their pipeline, he'll have them back in his pocket soon enough."

"They've thought this through that far?"

"No. The boys are just scared."

"Was it the other boy who shot Jimmy?"

"No. That much we do know. His parents can alibi him."

"That means Jimmy connected with the real dealer. You said Jimmy doesn't know him, but can he at least describe him?"

Hal shook his head then held out a hand, palm-out, to stop her next comment. "The guy seems to live in the shadows. And before you think I'm incompetent again, believe me. We've tried everything we know to get Jimmy—and the other boy—to tell us how he wound up behind the school with the shooter. But he won't talk."

"I wonder if I can get him to tell me…"

Hal went to object, but now it was Steph who held out a hand. "Listen to me. It's like that old cliché, 'the enemy of my enemy is my friend.' Jimmy knows everything that's happened here." She waved toward the pharmacy and then up and down the aisles. "And now he's been the target, too. I might be able to get him to commiserate, to share with me, simply because we're both at the mercy of the same creep—"

A horrible thought brought her up short. "You don't think we have more than one of them loose in town, do you?"

At first, Hal looked ready to comment. But then, after a few minutes of thought, he shrugged. "I don't know—on either count. There's a small chance it might work, but there's a greater chance he might dig in his heels even more. Let me think about it."

Steph wanted to lobby on, but since he hadn't shut her down right away, she figured she shouldn't push her luck. He might still come around and see the logic behind her plan. "Fine, then, Hal. You just let me know when you're done with all that thinking you still have to do."

He chuckled. "There's a lot more than meets the eye behind your quiet, hardworking pharmacist facade. I'm thinking you might have a hidden detective somewhere in there, Wonder Woman with a secret wish to interrogate."

"Boy, you sure know how to sweet-talk a girl."

His eyes widened at her comment, and she felt dumb. How could she have come up with something like that? Just because she was interested, and he had seemed equally so a couple of times, didn't mean she should have come out with that kind of potentially suggestive comment.

"I'm sorry," she said, blushing. "That was…oh, I don't know. I shouldn't have said something like that."

"There you go again, beating up on yourself. Didn't I tell you I have the market cornered on that? I do all the beating up around here. Trust me, it's enough for both of us."

She knew he'd brought that up just to make her feel better, and she was grateful, but she still felt dumb. It was time to head home—way past time, actually. Miss Tabitha probably had something delicious cooked up and ready to eat.

"Ah…it's time to lock up," she said, moving away. "I don't want Miss Tabitha to worry about me, and she does."

He gestured for her to precede him.

Steph locked the pharmacy door, now repaired—for a second time—then went out to the back stoop. She turned to lock up and nearly bumped into Hal.

"Whoa…"

His hands clasped her shoulders, and his warmth penetrated her jacket. Steph felt the strongest urge to just lean forward, to place her head on his chest, as she'd done at the hospital. The past few weeks had taken their toll, and even though she'd felt a momentary betrayal when she'd learned he hadn't told her everything he'd learned about her case, she knew Hal was a special man.

Oh, sure. He wasn't the kind in big-screen romances, the

Cary Grant or Rock Hudson slick hero with the perfect line at the drop of a hat. He didn't fit in with the image of the dream man she'd had when she decked out her home in ruffles and lace. Hal Benson was far better than those illusions she'd once formed.

He was a decent man, one who really cared about making a difference, in a job that put to use that powerful wish. He also had the kind of faith a woman could share, solid, firm and rooted in the knowledge of God's righteousness and blessings.

That was good. And bad.

She'd really gone and done it. As Steph looked up into Hal's face, the last auburn glow of the late autumn sunset around him, she finally admitted the truth.

She'd fallen in love with Hal Benson.

She closed her eyes and considered that truth for a moment, what it might mean, the possible joy and potential heartache she now faced. As she stood there and hovered between fear and excitement, Hal ran a finger down her cheek, along her jaw and to her chin. His gentle touch sent more of his warmth through her, warming her clear down to her heart. At the same time that same warmth set off a bubbling, a certain effervescence, that swirled up to her head…a happiness, almost giddiness. She felt feminine and treasured, both at the same time.

She met his gaze, and she realized he was about to kiss her. In that last second, she knew it was what she wanted, too. His lips touched hers with a tenderness that filled her with wonder. His arms eased around her, and he deepened the kiss. She felt cherished, and, returning the caress, infusing it with all the emotions bursting in her, hoping she could give back that same sense of joy he was giving her, she felt she never wanted to move away from his side.

"Hey, Steph! Are you ready— Oh! Sorry!"

At the sound of Winnie Zook's voice, Steph stumbled backward, pressing up against the metal handrail on the stoop. Hal's expression tightened for a moment; then he shrugged and gave her a wry smile.

"Busted!" he whispered, and then, stunning her, he winked.

That simple gesture broke through Steph's embarrassment. She chuckled. "I completely forgot I'd agreed to meet Winnie for supper at Granny Annie's and then for the three of us to ride to Bible study together. It's been quite a day." And then she decided to get up some gumption and face things squarely. "You do realize the whole town will know you... ah...we..."

Yeah, right. Gumption. She gave up and just waved vaguely. "You know."

Again, he winked. "Yeah, I know. It's called a kiss. And I don't mind if the whole world knows I just kissed you. Have a great supper and a satisfying Bible study."

He plopped his hat on his head, ran down the steps, tapped his hat brim in a jaunty salute for Winnie and then headed to the cruiser he'd parked at the entrance to the alley.

After he drove off, Steph looked at Winnie. And groaned.

The town's most dedicated gossip's eyes had widened to saucer size, her mouth gaped and she alternated looks in the direction Hal had taken and where Steph still stood.

She took a deep breath and slowly made her way down the steps. It was going to take her some time to get used to her brand-new status. She'd never had a "boyfriend" before. In the eyes of the town, and thanks to Winnie, she soon would.

How was that going to feel?

When Steph got back to her room in Miss Tabitha's house, her cell phone rang. She was tired and didn't really feel like talking to her parents, dodging questions, avoiding any comment that might further alarm them.

By now, of course, they'd heard at least some of what had happened at the store. Steph had spent an enormous amount of time and energy calming their fears.

But it wasn't Mom or Dad on the phone; it was Darcy.

"Hey!" she said. "What's up?"

"Are you out of your mind?" Darcy asked, her voice almost shrill. "Kissing Hal Benson behind your store?"

Okay, so what did she say now? It was bad enough to know the whole town was buzzing about that kiss—an amazing kiss, true, but it had never been meant for public dissection.

"Um…hi, Darcy. How was your day?"

"Cut it out, Stephanie Lou Scott. I mean it. Are you nuts?"

When Steph didn't answer, Darcy went on in her usual steamroller way. "He's a cop! Do you know what I'm saying? He's the cop who's investigating *you*. People are saying you're smooching him to get him off your case, and therefore you're guilty."

It was much worse than she'd thought. "That's stupid."

"*People* are stupid. So why help them with the stupid?"

"Give me a break, Darcy. It was just a kiss. You've got a whole conspiracy theory going there. And, really. It only happened a little while ago. You and the town's buzz machine have sure been busy at my expense, haven't you?"

"Look, I'm just worried about you."

Although Steph was irritated, she understood Darcy's concern. "Don't be. I'm okay."

"And what if *he's* the one doing the finagling? What if he's the one with the agenda? He could just be trying to get you all cozy and lovey-dovey and then get you to say something that sounds guilty. Are you ready to deal with that? Would you be okay with that, too?"

For the second time that day, Steph's thoughts of Hal took a downward turn. Had he thought the most direct way to an arrest went through her heart? Had he kissed her to smooth over her earlier suspicions? Was the man who seemed so honest and sincere really what he appeared?

"I'll be okay," she said again. "I'm trusting God, Darcy. He's in charge."

"I sure hope you're right." Her voice took on a decidedly dark tone. "Your God might be in control, but He's never been on my side, so for your sake, I really, really hope your experience isn't like mine."

Darcy's spiritual vacuum had always troubled Steph, but this was anything but the time to give another testimony of her faith. She curtailed her comment to a simple, "God's always on the side of those He loves, and that's everyone. We're the ones who stray or don't even come over to His side."

"Fine, Steph. You've told me all about it a whole bunch of times. But you know God's not the deal right now. The deal right now is making sure we keep you out of the slammer and in business."

Even though Steph knew Darcy was waiting for a response, she didn't have anything to say. What was there to say? She didn't want to wind up in jail any more than her best friend wanted her there.

Darcy went on. "My life's been no bed of roses, and you know it. But you? You've always been the one who's known what she wants, and you've gone for it. All this that's happened…well, it's terrible. I'm really sorry it's happened to you."

Steph thought she heard Darcy's voice hitch with a suppressed sob. "Thanks, but—"

"And I'm worried about what else might come your way," Darcy said as though she hadn't heard Steph. "I…I love you like the sister I don't have, and I can't stand the thought that you might wind up hurt for real. I…couldn't stand any of the ups and downs of life if I didn't do whatever I could to keep you safe."

"I love you, too, Darce. And I do mean it. I'm okay, really okay. Please don't worry. Just don't feed the gossip trolls, okay?" She kicked off her shoes and wiggled her toes. "You know what else? I'm beat. It was a tough day, and I just want to fill up the tub and soak for a while. Then I'm going to sleep. Let's talk again tomorrow."

Darcy's reluctant agreement was the best Steph was going to get, so they said goodbye. She gathered her bath basket, towel and fluffy white terry-cloth robe, and then she went to the big old-fashioned bath down the hall. As the water ran into the giant claw-foot tub, Darcy's questions returned to haunt her.

Could Hal really be as devious as Darcy thought?

Hal drove into his driveway to Pepper's barked greeting. He'd dropped by earlier to let her out, and they'd had a vigorous Frisbee game, the dog's favorite. Once he'd tired her out, he'd filled her kibble bowl and topped off her water before he'd headed out again.

Now it was dark. Even though he was tired, the dog had to relieve herself and burn off some more energy before she'd settle down for the night. He had to admit that even though he wanted to just plop in his chair and do nothing, the time he spent with Pepper never failed to raise his spirits and ease his mind out of cop mode.

A game with Pepper and a bunch of belly rubs and ear scratches would do them both a world of good. Then he could finally crash. Maybe he wouldn't be able to fall asleep right away, with all the thoughts zipping through his head, but that didn't really matter. Prayer and peace would suit him just fine.

The ringing doorbell soon told him that, as far as peace went, it wouldn't be coming any time soon. He opened the door to find Wayne Donnelly on his front porch. "I'm surprised. Is there a problem?"

"I don't know about a problem, exactly, but there is something I have to talk to you about."

Hal stepped aside. "Come on in, then." As they headed for the living room, he glanced over his shoulder. "Can I get you something to drink? I have cola, iced tea, water…"

"Water's fine."

Moments later, he returned, handed Wayne his drink and then sat in his armchair. Immediately, Pepper plopped at his feet, her disgusted sigh loud and heartfelt.

"So," Hal said after Wayne had taken a sip of water and put the glass down on the table at his side. "What's on your mind?"

"This isn't easy, you know?" The older cop averted his gaze and shook his head. "But there's no gettin' around it. I gotta say it and say it quick. This ain't the time for you to be going all sweet over Steph Scott. The gossip's blazing through town. It's not going to do you any favors."

Hal clenched his jaw. How did one justify following his heart? How did he tell another law enforcement officer that he knew in that very same heart that Steph wasn't involved?

"It's okay, Wayne. I'm well aware of the situation."

Wayne arched a graying brow. "Don't know if you really are. I'm afraid you're letting yourself get blinded by nothing more than a pretty face. She's in a bad situation, and she wouldn't be the first woman to play a man. Especially the man whose job it is to get the goods on her."

"There are no 'goods' to get on Steph, man. She's innocent."

"See? That's what I mean." Wayne shook his head again. "I'm afraid—and so's the chief—that she's playing you to protect her hide. You got a lot at stake here."

He was supposed to let them lock Steph up for a crime she hadn't committed just to save himself? His job?

"Look, I can't deny I…care for Steph. I have for a long time. But I also can't let you forget that we have nothing, absolutely no evidence, to charge her with anything. She has nothing to do with drugs, nothing, you understand?"

"Hal, think about your job, the campaign, your reputation!" Wayne stood and began to pace. "A man's only got one thing in the end, and that's his integrity. Don't let a flirtation compromise that."

Hal rose, too. He'd had enough. "I won't. Now, if you don't mind, it's been a long day, and I'm really looking forward to a long, hot shower. Bed's also looking pretty good right now."

He knew Wayne wanted to pursue his argument, but in the end, the cop nodded and headed for the front door. There, he took the old brass latch, opened it, then turned to glance back at Hal.

"Just think about what I said, okay?"

"Won't be able not to." He sighed. "And, Wayne? Thanks. I know you care, and I appreciate it."

On his way out, Wayne nodded.

Hal went upstairs, turned the water full on to Hot and tried to wash away the stress of the day.

But after he'd dried off and donned clean sweats, when he went to turn off the bathroom light, he caught sight of his face in the mirror.

"Is Wayne right? Is Steph really playing me for a fool?"

FOURTEEN

Loganton's gossips were having a field day at his and Steph's expense. While that irritated Hal plenty, what bothered him most was the growing rumble for the write-in ballot. It didn't help one bit that he knew Ethan wanted nothing of the sheriff's position.

Hal had flat out asked.

Ethan had said that he was done with field work. His too-close encounter with a bullet, thanks to a drug dealer, had made the decision for him. But what difference would Ethan's preference make if the movement grew to the point where he was elected? Once he refused to fill the position, those who'd voted for Ethan wouldn't want to see Hal in the job again.

On the other hand, there was little enthusiasm for Ed Townsend's candidacy. A very good thing.

The very worst thing, though, was Hal's cowardice. He hadn't been able to make himself face Steph since the evening he'd kissed her. Well, she'd been just as much an active participant in that kiss as he had, but he had taken the initiative to start the moment.

Truth be told, Wayne's visit had put the brakes on any further impulsive action. Not only did Hal not want to lose the election but also, and more to the point, he didn't want

Steph to have to face the town's running commentary. She didn't need any more negativity in her life. Being a drug dealer's target was more than enough.

So Hal had taken to checking on the pharmacy a number of times each night, taking his first pass after he knew she'd left. That was how he happened to find himself out back in the alley, once again looking at the replacement door lock, the multiunit electric junction box that juiced her surveillance system and then rounding the building to check the door out front. Had he not made a habit of this, he might have missed the latest spate of vandalism—if one could call it that.

The two exterior, long-range cameras out back had been jammed with wires, heavy-duty rubber bands and a pair of sticks. They no longer could swivel to scan the length of the alley. And while he couldn't say when it had been done, he did know nothing had happened at the store since the Fall Fest.

At least nothing illegal had happened. A new pharmacist had started on the job. Steph was struggling to make ends meet. She didn't discuss that aspect of her situation, but Hal had a good idea of what she was facing.

On the other hand, weeks had gone by since the last theft; conceivably the dealer was running low on ingredients. Attention had died down in town.

What were the odds against tonight being the time the perp had chosen for the next event? Was Hal willing to risk letting him get away with another break-in?

It seemed the perfect time to strike again.

He couldn't risk ignoring the signs.

He also couldn't see leaving Steph out of the loop.

Reluctantly, he pulled out his cell phone and dialed her number. When she answered, he realized how much he'd missed her during these days of self-imposed separation. He reminded himself he couldn't let his deepest feelings interfere with what he had to do.

"Steph? It's Hal. Where are you right now?"

A moment's silence. Then, "I'm at Miss Tabitha's, about to sit down to eat. Why?"

He sighed. There it was again, that pesky and too-frequent meal delay he went through every time he got a call as he was about to sit down to eat. He knew, though, what to suggest. "Are you willing to ask her to set aside a plate for you? There's something you need to see."

"What? What's going on?"

"I'm in the alley behind your store. Please come meet me here. You can explain to Miss Tabitha, but it's best if you don't make much of it as far as the other boarders go."

Another pause. "I'll be there in fifteen minutes."

He must have looked at his watch fifty times while he waited for Steph. Years of experience told him something was about to happen; expensive surveillance systems didn't get jammed, with wires, all on their own. All that experience of his also told him Steph would not be willing to be left out of anything related to the store from here on out.

Which proved to be the case the minute she showed up.

"Well, there's only one thing to do," she said once he showed her what he'd found. "We're just going to have to wait for him inside. I know we'll catch him then."

That was the response he'd expected, if not the one he'd wanted. He'd wanted her to disarm the alarm to the PD, turn over the key and go back to Miss Tabitha's while he did what he had to do. "We? What we?"

She pointed at him then at herself. "There's two of us here. That equals we."

He'd expected that, too. But he still had to try to keep her safe.

"In some other universe." He crossed his arms and spread his feet to brace himself. She was no pushover. "What *we're* going to do is this—you're going to disarm the alarm, hand over your keys and then go back to Miss Tabitha's. I'm going to go in, make myself comfortable for the night and wait for your thief to show up. Then I'm going to slap cuffs on him, alert my back-up when I've got the perp and hand him over for processing."

"In your dreams." She crossed her arms, too. "The last time, I gave you a pass. This time? No way. It's my store. You want the key? I come with it. *We* will make ourselves comfortable, and *we* will wait for the…perp to show up."

And he'd thought he liked the no-pushover version of Steph Scott. Hah!

Then again, had she ever been a pushover? Or was it more a case that he hadn't known her well enough to know how she'd react in a particular situation?

More importantly, how did he feel about her refusal to leave? How was he going to do his job and keep her safe at the same time? If only he didn't care so much…

"Steph, it won't be safe here for you. This guy's not shy about using a gun. I can't let you risk your safety, and if I'm to get this right, I won't be able to protect you *and* subdue him."

"I don't need to be babysat, Hal. You do your job, and I'll help you. I won't get in your way, but I also am not going to be shoved aside again. This store represents the past five years of my life, and it's also my future." She blew a stray strand of blond hair from an eyebrow then gave him a determined, level stare. "If you were in my place, you wouldn't leave, either. And you know I'm right."

He had nothing to say to that. She was right.

Something told him he was going to regret this. "Fine. But you have to listen to me. Don't argue every time I tell you to do something—just do it. Your life might depend on it."

"I won't do anything stupid, and getting in your way would be more than stupid."

He nodded but said nothing more. Instead, he called the Loganton PD and spoke to Wayne. Wayne and Maggie would be more than happy to offer backup, only needing a phone call to bring them from where they would set up surveillance at Monique's Mane Management, the salon four doors down and across the street from the drugstore. The only thing Hal failed to do, and he prayed he wouldn't come to regret it, was tell the two officers he wouldn't be alone.

With their lingering suspicion of her, and after all that gossip about the two of them, they'd never let Steph anywhere near the store during a stakeout.

When he hung up, Steph slipped the key into the lock. "There's no reason to wait out here any longer, is there?"

"I don't think so. It wouldn't make much sense to tip him off by hanging around outside."

After they went in, Hal checked out the whole store. Nothing seemed to have been disturbed. The interior cameras were still working, the alarm system activated but the laser system at the front door turned off, as Steph had left them earlier in the evening, and the pharmacy door hadn't been tampered with since she'd last had it fixed.

"Any spot better than another for us to hang out?" he asked.

She shrugged. "As long as he can't see us the minute he walks in, I don't think it matters."

He walked around, checking out the angle from different spots in relationship to the back door. He noticed the angle of the light that came in the front window, the darkest aisles versus those in the glow from the streetlight, and finally chose the pet products aisle as the place with the best view. "Come and join me. We'll hang out here to wait."

They sat on the floor, leaning against twenty-pound sacks of dog food. The doggy scent made Hal think of Pepper and the punishment she would deliver when he returned home. Still, he was glad she was there, waiting for him, ready to love him enough so he could let go of the stress of the day. Steph didn't even have a Pepper of her own.

"I seem to remember hearing you were taking in one of Miss Tabitha's cats," he said. "How's that going?"

"The kittens aren't old enough yet, but, yes, I've chosen a little girl. She's the sweetest ball of silver fluff."

He snorted. "From what I hear, if she's anything like her mother, there won't be much that's sweet about her. Why'd you decide on a cat instead of a dog?"

"I do want a living, breathing warm friend when I get home at night, but my hours wouldn't be fair to a dog. Cats are more independent, and a litter box solves one of the biggest pet problems that face a working person."

"Wish I could teach my greyhound to use a box. She's a pretty demanding housemate, but she's also great company. Wouldn't trade her for any snooty cat."

She wrinkled her nose. "That's not a nice way to see things. The way I see it, it's the companionship that matters. An empty house gets old pretty quick. The first three years after I came home and opened the store, my parents still lived here. But then they chose to downsize near Charlotte, and I've been on my own ever since. I think a kitten's a great idea."

He knew what they were both saying…without saying it straight out. And he refused to let cowardice cheat them out of the chance at something wonderful. "Steph…about the other night—"

His phone rang. It was the dispatcher. "Benson here."

He listened for a few minutes, frustration growing. "Fine. But I'm on a stakeout. Can't the guys handle it until I'm done here—"

The dispatcher was not happy. She grew insistent. Hal gave in to the inevitable. "All right, all right. I'll be there."

"What's wrong?" Steph asked when he hung up.

"A major wreck out on the highway just got called in. Ambulance, fire trucks, the whole thing. I need to be there." He stood, held out a hand to help her up. "Let's go. We'll just have Wayne and Maggie keep an eye on what goes down out here."

She pulled her hand back and stood on her own. "I'm going nowhere. I'll see you…" She waved. "Whenever."

Hal couldn't believe what he was hearing. "I don't think you understand. I've got to go out to the highway and work an accident scene. You can't stay here alone."

"Of course I can—"

"This guy's already mugged you. He shot up a wedding. Do you have a death wish?"

"Of course not. But I don't want my store robbed again, either."

"And what do you intend to do when he walks in?"

"I intend to call 911. You've alerted the PD. They're expecting trouble here. You know I can call them when I need help. I'll be fine."

"That's crazy. Of course, you won't be fine. You'll be begging for a bullet between the brows. You can't stay by yourself." When her expression only turned more stubborn, his frustration grew. "Come on, Steph. You know this is crazy. I can have Wayne and Maggie split up and one watch the back and the other the front door. The perp won't try anything. You and I can try this again tomorrow."

"Don't you think Wayne and Maggie will tip him off for real? He's not going to try again tomorrow if we do that. Go ahead and work your crime scene—it is your job. I'll stay and protect mine."

"Look—"

"No, you look. My business is as important to me as your job is to you. Like I said, go do your job. Your constituents expect it of you, and they're watching, especially during an election. Don't risk your career."

He tightened his fists, trying to control his rising fear—and frustration. "And yet you think I should let you risk your life?"

"I won't risk my life. I'll call for help."

"But—"

His phone rang again. He flipped it open and growled, "Yeah?"

The dispatcher again. He had to go. A look at Steph made him groan. "I really didn't want to do this, but I'm going to pull rank on you. I'm the sheriff. You can't stay here alone. It wouldn't be the smartest move. If I have to, I'll…" He took a deep breath. "I'll put you under arrest."

Shock blanched her features, so much so he could see it in the dim light around them. She looked as though he'd punched her in the gut. Hal suspected she felt he'd betrayed her. But he hadn't. He'd only done what he knew he had to do. Wayne and Maggie would have to be enough.

She stood, silent and stiff. A sharp nod was his only response. With quick steps, she hurried to the back door, opened up, switched the alarm back on and stepped outside.

"Steph…"

The glare she gave him cut off his attempt to smooth things over. He might have just blown any chance he had for pursuing a relationship with her, but at least he could now rest easy about her safety. He'd rather she live and walk away from him than die in a misguided show of courage and obstinacy.

He drew a deep breath. "I'll be in touch."

The look she slanted his way should have had daggers hitting him. "You do that, Sheriff Benson. Hopefully before you and yours drag me off to jail or make some other *stupid* move that puts the final nail in my future's coffin."

He'd really done it. He'd obviously touched the ADD nerve. She'd mentioned how she'd had to fight the "stupid" label all the way through school. She wasn't stupid. He knew that. But this time she'd made a rotten decision, and in his fear for her safety, he'd blurted out without giving his words any thought. Still, she would have been in incalculable danger, and Hal couldn't have protected her. He would have to count on Wayne and Maggie.

And God.

It was going to test the strength of his faith, since he couldn't do the job himself.

Hal flicked on the cherry light and slapped it to the roof of the cruiser. He then jumped in and tore out of the parking lot on the other side of the street from the drugstore. With Steph pulling that stubborn mule routine back there, the sooner he wrapped up the accident scene, the sooner he could return to the store. He might still have a chance to catch the thief.

He had no other recourse. He had to answer the accident call. But he could pray.

"Father, please be with her. She's got a great attitude and

all the heart a woman could want. I'm not trying to diminish her, just keep her safe. And do my job. This guy we're after has no trouble using a gun. Steph's no match for him."

He drove out of town, snippets of conversation bouncing against memories in his head. Whoever had picked her for a target hadn't known she'd fight back. Had the intention been to run her out of business? Or had the perp thought she'd let him go on and on, helping himself to whatever ingredients he wanted for his witches' brew? Only a defeatist would have taken that route.

Steph was anything but defeated.

Right about now, Hal would have liked a little defeat on her part. Instead, he had a feisty woman ready to give back as good as she got. But she had only a pair of cops a hundred yards and a street's width away as a hedge between her store and disaster. He understood how hard it was to walk away.

He'd just had to do the same thing. With her.

He hoped his guys were already out at the accident, taking care of the scene, doing their usual and excellent investigative job, so he could get back to the store—

No. He had to be honest. He wanted to hurry back to Steph. He wanted to wrap his arms around her, promise her he'd protect her and her store, but he couldn't do that. Even once the accident was cleared away.

Thinking and praying, Hal reached the mile marker the dispatcher had mentioned, and found…nothing.

He pulled over to the shoulder and used his phone rather than the radio to call back in. Something didn't feel right, and there were too many CB fans running around these days. "Where did you say I'd find the wreck?"

The dispatcher went over the directions again.

Hal backed up to the last marker he'd passed. He hadn't

made a mistake. There was nothing there. "Didn't you say the guys needed my help? Looks like they're done."

"We got another call. I sent one unit to respond to that one, but the other should be there."

"There's no one here. The other unit probably went to help with that second call when they got here and found nothing. Where'd they go?"

"A fire at a farm out on Willow Hill Road—a fatality there. Possible arson. The fire department's on the scene, too." She paused, and Hal heard a tapping as she thought. "Aren't the EMTs there with the victims?"

He no longer felt something was wrong—he *knew* it. "I don't think you understood what I said. There's no one here— no accident, no cars, no victims, no ambulance, no deputies. I'm the only person on the side of the road."

"No ambulance? I'll have to follow up on that. Still…"

His patience was running out. "Still…?"

"Could they have beat you to the accident, taken care of everything and headed back to headquarters? I don't know, Sheriff. It sure sounds crazy—or like a totally sick joke."

As soon as the young woman uttered the last word, Hal knew. He knew exactly what had happened. "Get the phone company in on this. Have them track that accident call. This was nothing more than a hoax. I'm willing to stake my career and my reputation on it. And you'd better send everyone you can round up to Scott's Pharmacy in Loganton. I don't care how many fires we're dealing with. It looks like we're also dealing with another drug theft."

Hal knew he was right. He also knew his earlier suspicion was correct. They were jousting with a pro. But maybe, just maybe, they could turn the tables on him tonight.

If the Lord so willed.

He spun his tires, kicking up gravel and dirt against the undercarriage of his cruiser, turned around and headed back to Loganton. He hit the direct dial function on his cell phone and called Wayne Donnelly. Who didn't answer.

Again.

A voice-mail message would have to do. A few curt words later, Hal hung up and floored the gas pedal.

He'd thought he was a step ahead of the thief by arranging for Wayne and Maggie to stake out the store. Now, he wasn't so sure. Of anything.

Wayne better pick up that message. And soon. Or things were on their way to worse than anyone could have envisioned.

In spite of the late hour, Hal turned on the siren. He didn't want to slow down for traffic.

Steph's future was at stake.

FIFTEEN

After Hal had left, Steph had driven three blocks away from the store, where she'd parked. Now, she had to wait until she was sure he wouldn't come back to check on her. That would make for a confrontation she didn't want to have. It'd be best if he finished whatever it was a sheriff had to do at a bad crash on a highway before they saw each other again.

It wouldn't be long. She knew the perp would strike soon. So she was going back. To the store. She couldn't let the thief get away with more of the components he needed to cook up his poisonous products. A quick call to 911, as she'd told Hal, would bring help as soon as she needed it.

Moments later, she let herself into the store.

It was dark, but through the front window, she could see the glow from the streetlight at the corner. It illuminated a patch near the front, leaving the windowless side and the rear of the store in the dark. She would hide near the pharmacy, in the pet aisle, close to the front. The thief would come in the door she'd just locked behind her.

The only change in the plan was Hal's absence at her side.

From where she hid, she wouldn't be able to see the perp's face, but she would know the moment he entered the store. At the thought, everything inside her did a flip. As nervous as she was, she couldn't wait to identify the person who'd targeted her. She couldn't wait to put an end to the siege. She couldn't wait until life went back to the way it had been before the night she was mugged—

No! She wanted life back to the way it had been before she found the first vandalized item. Her problems hadn't started with the mugging. She was sure.

A car drove by out front. In contrast, the silence inside the store seemed thick, oppressive, overwhelming.

Steph glanced at her watch again. To her dismay, it only showed a brief nine minutes had gone by since she'd sat against the sack of kibble. Even though her watch was electronic, she could almost hear time ticking by. She certainly heard the beat of her heart. Her breathing seemed louder than the rush of wind before a thunderstorm.

The old building creaked.

She jerked to hair-trigger alert.

When nothing more happened, she forced herself to use her common sense and relax. Well, she consciously tried to relax, but she was too shaky—the results of the adrenaline rush the impending danger, her stealthy return and the loud creak had set off. Sometimes being a pharmacist was a pain. She really didn't want to know what her body was doing right then. She wanted the thief to arrive, the PD to arrest him, the judicial system to try and convict him and then the prison system to lock him up and throw away the key. And she wanted it all to happen fast.

It would have been so much easier to make it through the night if Hal hadn't had to leave. She missed him. Sure, his solid, steady presence and his law enforcement training had made her aware of the protection he afforded her. But her wish to see him came from more than just the sake of safety.

She missed him for him.

She wanted to hear him talk about Pepper again. She wanted to hear more about his feelings, about his choice of a career in law enforcement instead of research or medicine, rocket science or architecture. She wanted to know why he'd come back to Loganton when she knew the whole world had been literally his for the taking because of his intelligence, diligence and talent.

She wanted to know everything there was to know about Hal Benson, the man. Hal Benson the sheriff was impressive; she was in love with the man.

Another creak.

Steph's stomach knotted. Her hearing seemed to sharpen to a painful point. Her back itched, but she didn't dare move, even to scratch. The tip of her nose…it tickled. She felt a sneeze coming on.

Was he there? Had the thief finally arrived?

She strained to hear. But nothing. The silence grew.

Her heart pounded, and she felt queasy, nauseated. She might as well face the truth. She was scared, more scared than she'd ever been before.

Had Hal been right? Was she being stubborn and stupid? Should she have listened to him and gone on home when he left?

Then she heard it. A metallic *click*. From the rear of the store.

Had the thief had yet another key made? Or had he come up with a set of locksmith's tools to break in? Was it even the thief?

Might it be Hal?

A thin sliver of light outlined the edges of the door. Steph always kept the hinges well-oiled, so it made no sound as it opened farther. She took a breath, held it, watched.

A cold blast of wind came in with the intruder. As the gust blew past her, Steph caught the slightest hint of fragrance, a familiar scent, spicy and vaguely sweet. She sniffed, again, and then it struck her.

This was what she'd struggled to remember for so long. The mugger had borne a whiff of this fragrance when he'd attacked her. She smothered the groan that threatened to escape. Might they have identified the person if she'd remembered sooner?

The door slid closed again. A figure took shape, blacker still than the surrounding dark. Steph strained to make out details, anything to offer the police, but all she could see was the intruder's shadowy bulk.

She kept staring as the figure came closer to the pharmacy area, but no matter how hard she tried, she couldn't make out more than its human form. Male or female, thin or fat; she couldn't see anything that might offer the authorities any help in identifying the thief.

Except the scent. It grew stronger as the intruder approached. It also grew more familiar with every passing second, teasing her memory yet staying just beyond its reach.

In the silent darkness, Steph waited, praying, poised for action.

What should she do? Should she jump out to try to startle the thief? Would she be able to catch him off guard? If she did catch him off guard…then what? Could she overpower him? She didn't feel particularly powerful right then. Or should she just wait until the cops got there—

Great. She'd been so caught up in the moment that she hadn't thought to call 911. She couldn't risk being overheard right then. She was on her own.

But not alone. God was with her. He would be enough.

She took a deep breath and stood. That scent…

The thief took a step closer.

Steph moved forward.

So did the thief.

With a quick prayer and all the courage she could muster, she launched herself at the intruder, ripped off the hoodie and identified the fragrance. Gum!

Pain, betrayal, dismay, shock…

A cry: "No! Father God…why?"

Darcy's face glowed pale in the dark. The gun in her hand shone steely and grim.

Hal's tires squealed as he took the next corner. "Easy now. Slow down, pal." He held the cell phone at his ear. "Come on, come on, come *on!*"

Why didn't Wayne pick up? Why would he not answer when he knew the store was about to be robbed again? Had he picked up the voice mail? Could Wayne and Maggie have already gone across the street? Had the thief shown up? Could they be slapping cuffs on him right then?

In his dreams, maybe. Something told Hal things hadn't gone that way at all.

He pushed the gas pedal, but it went no farther. The car was at its limit. Still, Hal refused to think of all the speed limits he was breaking. He slowed down enough to keep the cruiser under control. His siren blared.

The night had been well planned. But not by him.

The perp had stayed one step ahead the whole time.

His phone rang. "Yeah?"

"Donnelly, here. We got a call to a fire on Willow Hill Road. We figured we might as well go, since we'd seen you leave the store. Didn't think much would happen since you'd decided to abort."

"I got called to a wreck on the highway. Turned out to be

a hoax. I'm almost back at the pharmacy, and I need backup. I'm sure he's either in already or on his way. Hoaxes don't happen out of the blue."

"Be right there."

He slapped the phone shut, hoping the partners did get there right away. Although he was more than ready to confront Steph's tormentor, he wasn't crazy enough to try to do it alone.

Unless he had no other choice.

He'd grudgingly agreed to let Steph stay with him knowing Wayne and Maggie would be only yards away. He'd sent her home, counting on his PD colleagues. But things had changed. Now, he didn't know what he'd face when he got to the store.

Thinking back to when he and Steph had parted—in anger— he couldn't help but groan. She'd locked up again, turned the security alarm back on. He didn't have the key or the code.

Well, too bad. He didn't care. The way things had played out, he was ready to shoot the doorknob, the lock—whatever it took to get inside. He was going in, and he'd deal with the consequences later. The perp hadn't aborted his plans.

He skidded on his next turn. "Whoa!"

He had to slow down. He couldn't very well blaze into the drugstore like some kind of latter-day Rambo, blinded by his feelings. That would only gain him a burst of gunfire as a greeting. If the intruder had made it in.

If not, he'd have some explaining to do for shooting a door.

Once in the parking lot across the side street by Scott's, Hal jumped out and pulled his gun from the holster. Weapon in hand, he approached the alley, his senses on high alert.

Everything looked like it had when he left a half hour earlier. He heard nothing other than a car that drove down Main Street. The lighting in the alley was as dim as always, and the reek from the Dumpster as pungent as ever.

He approached the back door slowly, his eyes sweeping every inch of the alley. With a quick prayer, he took hold of the door latch. As it gave, he realized he'd been half expecting it to do just that.

His instincts hadn't let him down.

His Lord wouldn't either. "Help me, Father."

Moving forward by millimeters, he opened the door just enough to slip inside. Just as carefully, he closed up again. That's when he heard the voices.

One was Steph's.

He should have known she'd come back.

Since he hadn't been willing to consider the possibility of harm coming to her, he'd wanted to believe she'd stay out of danger.

She hadn't.

As he stepped closer, his anger on the rise, a heart-stopping sight met his gaze. Two women, tears gleaming in the light from the lamp outside, stood no more than five feet from each other. But it wasn't sheer distance that kept them apart.

The gun in Darcy's hand did that.

"Why?" Steph said again, her voice thick with emotion. "Why would you do this to me? Why would you throw me off the back step? Why would you attack me?"

"Please," Darcy begged. "Don't make it any harder than it already has been. Give me the key to the pharmacy door. Don't make me hurt you. No matter what's happened, I never wanted to do that."

Steph's head swam. Nothing made sense. "How could you get mixed up with drugs? When did you start using? How did you get hooked?"

Darcy reared back as though Steph had slapped her. "I don't do drugs. You ought to know that."

"Then why? Why are you in my store, in the middle of the night, holding a gun on me—*me!*"

With a jerky gesture, Darcy waved the gun, shrugged and sobbed. "You wouldn't understand. You haven't had to deal with…stuff like I have."

"Come on, Darcy. Put that thing down. Don't make matters worse. If it goes off, you don't know what you might hit. And you said you didn't want to hurt me."

All her plea did was make Darcy aim the weapon more squarely at Steph. "Give me the key, then. I'll take the stuff and split. No more gun, no more hassle."

Steph knew she couldn't give Darcy the key to the pharmacy, but she didn't want to force her friend's hand and let her think she had no other choice but to shoot. What had happened to Darcy, the Darcy she'd known all her life?

"Okay," she said, praying for wisdom, the right thing to say. "You've got the gun, but I have the questions. Give me something here. Help me understand. What's gone wrong? You know no one's life is perfect. What's so bad with yours that you would think you have to do this?"

"You wouldn't understand—"

"That's the second time you said that. Try me. You've always told me everything before. I don't remember you complaining about my lack of understanding."

"This is different."

"How?"

"You're not going to let it go, are you?"

When Steph bit her bottom lip and shook her head, Darcy chuckled without any humor. "I should have known."

"You know me. I thought I knew you. Please talk to me."

"You're the last one who'll get where I'm coming from. You with your perfect life, your perfect family, your perfect store. You haven't had to fight the world just to keep on going."

"Hey! I'm the one with the ADD, the learning disability, remember? I've had my share of fighting to do."

Darcy rolled her eyes. Steph thought back to their childhood. "I know it wasn't easy growing up without your dad, but after he died, your mom was great…"

Anger twisted Darcy's features. "You didn't have to see her die a little each day after she got sick. The pain was so bad…the cancer…" She shrugged.

"I know taking care of her was tough on you, and I admire the strength you showed—"

"Tough doesn't even come close. We had no money to cover the treatments—sure, there was insurance, but the deductibles and maximums we had to pay ourselves are killers. We sold her car, lost the house and I couldn't go and get myself started on a decent career. I needed money—more, more, *more*—just to keep her alive as long as I could."

More tears drenched Steph's face. "Why didn't you come to us? You should have known we would help. Mom and Dad always loved you, and I would have done whatever I could. I even gave you her meds."

"We couldn't drag you guys down with us. And Mama wouldn't let me tell, anyway. She…she had her pride."

Steph winced. Pride. Mixed with need. "But she died a year ago. Why all this now?"

The bark of a laugh Darcy gave grated on Steph's heart. "Now? Because once you're in, you can't get out. And I had too many debts to finish paying off."

Steph's brain struggled to process all the information Darcy was sending her way. "You're in…and you can't get out. That means you're not alone in this, are you?"

Averting her gaze from Steph's, Darcy shrugged.

"Who? Who's got you doing this?"

"Doesn't matter, Steph. All that matters is the key. Hand it over, so I can get out of here. I'll…I'll never bother you again."

Darcy might never steal from her again, but the grief from this encounter would never leave Steph. She didn't know how to make her friend see that truth. But she might be able to stall her long enough for Hal to come back from his accident on the road.

She spread her hands. "Look. It's me, Darcy. You can tell me what's going on. Who's behind this? Who's making the meth?"

"That, I can answer. I don't know who's making the meth."

Steph's mind scrambled the images and the words, still trying to make sense of it all. "You don't know who's making the drug, but you must know whoever it is you say has a grip on you. Why would you put yourself in even more trouble just to protect a creep like that?"

When Darcy looked away again, Steph knew. "It's someone you care for…a guy! You fell in love with the wrong one. Oh, Darce—"

"Stop with that 'Oh, Darce' deal, will you? I don't need pity, I just need the key—"

"You don't need pity, but you do need mercy. And love. The real thing, Darcy. The kind of love that lasts, that you can always count on."

As Steph watched the emotions play over her friend's face, she caught the hint of movement beyond Darcy's head. Was that the accomplice? The guy who'd stuck his claws into her heart and brought her down?

Steph squared her shoulders. What she had to say didn't

change. It was always the same, no matter who heard it, who spoke it or who took hold of the truth.

"You need the love God offers you. He's been waiting for you forever. All you have to do is say yes."

Darcy's sob nearly broke Steph's heart. "It's too late for me. It's been too late for a long time. That's why it's best if you give me the key. I'll get paid, and I'll get out of your life. I won't bother anyone else again."

Frustration threatened but Steph refused to give up on her friend when Darcy needed her most. "I want you to stay. I want to help you through whatever you have to face. Your friendship—*you*—mean too much to me. And to God. Don't lose hope. I don't hold any of this against you, and the Lord loves you so much, He was willing to die for you."

Steph knew the moment she chipped a chink in Darcy's armor. Her best friend's hand, the one with the gun, shook. She pressed on. "You don't still love this guy, do you? Because you know he never loved you. Love doesn't force you into crime. He took advantage of your situation, of your pain."

Darcy shrugged.

Her lack of argument spoke volumes. "Miss Tabitha loves you. I love you. Mom and Dad love you. That's more than many people have going for them. You'll have to deal with the consequences of what you've done, but we'll all help."

"You can't. I've done too much to even hope for anything—"

"You're alive, Darcy. There's always hope while there's life. Even for a killer—" The memory of the bullets flying past her came back in full. "Did you shoot Granny Annie and Jimmy?"

Horror burst on Darcy's freckled face. "Of course not! I would never do that."

"Then that's a plus on your side. If you help the police

get the jerk who used you, you'll chalk up more points in your favor—"

"They already have him!"

As soon as the words left Darcy's lips, she gasped. She hadn't meant to reveal that much. Then the strength seemed to seep from her. She sagged. She lowered the hand with the gun.

"He's behind bars," she said in little more than a whisper. "But I still owed him. And he's got friends…they wouldn't let me stop."

"You can stop now," Steph said. "You can walk into God's open arms at any time. He's waiting for you, Darce. Just like me. I'm waiting for you to stop the craziness and get started on the rest of your life."

She held out her arms to her friend.

Darcy's hand shook again; she took a step forward. Steph caught her breath.

But then her friend drew in a rough breath and squared her shoulders. "No. It's too late. Give me—"

A pair of muscular male arms came around from behind Darcy. The black shadow Steph had spotted at the back of the store materialized into Hal. Darcy let out a cry like that of a wounded animal. She tossed her head, her hair a tangled mass that swirled over her face.

Hal held tight.

The gun fell to the floor.

Steph's tears flowed unchecked as a sob ripped from her throat. She stared at the gun in horror. How could this possibly be? How could Darcy have let herself get caught up in this mess?

"How," Steph whispered. "How could you have done this to me?"

Wayne Donnelly and Maggie Lowe walked in, weapons drawn, intense concentration on their faces. When Darcy saw the guns in the police officers' hands, she quit fighting Hal. All her strength seemed to leave her, and she sagged back against him.

A pair of shiny handcuffs snicked into place. The officers took their prisoner away. Betrayal burned in Steph's heart.

But then Hal approached, a smile full of emotion on his handsome face. Steph met his gaze. "It's over," she said.

"You put an end to the siege."

The weeks that followed flew by in a whirlwind of activity. Steph had never known days so full, emotions so intense. Darcy faced the full force of the law for breaking and entering, theft of a controlled substance and vandalism. It turned out she'd used the tissue box and the other items to hide the money she'd made for the drug boss to retrieve. She insisted she'd never seen the man but rather picked up her instructions—and the drug she couriered to individual dealers every so often—from several hiding places around town. The drugstore was only one drop-off spot. She seemed certain the mastermind wasn't local. She insisted she had no idea who she'd dealt with.

The man who'd captured her heart was the man Ethan Rodgers had busted months before. He'd insisted they keep their relationship secret until, as he'd told her, he was in a position to propose—with a ring. Steph offered Darcy a shoulder to cry on, a willing and sympathetic ear and answered a multitude of questions about her faith.

In exchange for a slightly shortened sentence, Darcy would cooperate with the authorities as they continued to search for the mastermind behind the scenes.

Ethan and Tess returned from their honeymoon, and Ethan publicly addressed those who'd wanted to elect him to the sheriff's job. He didn't want it, wouldn't accept it. He would, however, take the Loganton PD chief's job when Bruce Zacharias turned in his badge January first.

That just left the contest between Ed Townsend and Hal Benson to be won. Its outcome had only grown in importance for Steph since the night of Darcy's arrest.

As the officers had led her friend away, Steph had fallen into Hal's arms, sobbing, her heart heavy and aching. Hal had just held her; his strong arms had cradled her until her grief had left her drained and without another tear to shed.

Since then, they'd spent hours and hours together. Steph had taken over Granny Annie's job as campaign manager while the older woman recovered from her gunshot wound.

And now, Election Day had come and was almost gone. Steph voted early then spent the rest of the day at the church's fellowship hall, putting together Hal's victory party. No one gave serious consideration to the possibility of a loss.

Red, white and blue bunting decked the stage. Crepe paper streamers in the same colors swooped from the central light fixture to the four corners and all four walls. A long table sagged under the weight of the food offered by Hal's supporters, and the church's punch fountain bubbled over with a tangy, orange juice–based drink.

All the campaign workers had gathered, waiting for the candidate to arrive from work and for the results to be announced. None waited more anxiously than Steph.

She and Hal had been practically inseparable since the night of Darcy's arrest, and not just to work on his campaign. They'd gone on as many dates as Hal's busy schedule allowed them to and talked for hours on end.

As close as they'd become, as much as Steph's love for Hal had grown, he hadn't tried to kiss her again. She hoped she hadn't misread the interest in his eyes. If she had, she was in for a world of hurt. And because she wasn't interested in playing at relationships, she'd decided to come right out and ask. Tonight, after he won the election and was in a good mood, she'd address the issue.

While she couldn't wait to see him again, she also dreaded the moment he walked in. She wasn't looking forward to hearing him say he didn't share her feelings. But if that were the case, she'd be better off knowing now.

A loud cheer rang out. Steph turned and saw Hal walk in, still in uniform, hat in hand. He scanned the crowd, and when he met her gaze, he winked then smiled. Although many wanted to shake his hand, he made progress and before long stood in front of her.

"Well?" she asked. "What do exit polls say?"

He shrugged then winked. "The word *landslide*'s been used a time or two."

She grinned. "We did it!"

"We sure did." He looked around, held out his hand. "Can you spare me a minute?"

Uh-oh! First the wink; now he'd turned serious. What was going on?

Was he going to beat her to "the talk"? And if so, which way was it going to go?

Fighting down her inner coward, Steph nodded and took hold. "The kitchen's empty, last I checked. All the food's out here, and the punch refills are, too."

His brows drew close, but then he shrugged. "It won't take long."

That's when she really started to worry.

In the kitchen, he let the door close behind them. He set down his hat, turned to face her and then, before he spoke a single word, he smoothed a strand of bangs off her forehead with the tip of his index finger. A tingle of pleasure rushed right to her head.

He placed his hands on her shoulders and drew her close. So far so good.

"Steph—"

"Hal—"

They chuckled, and she was glad to note his chuckle was as nervous as hers.

He shook his head. "Look, I'm not the kind with a million pretty words or a sixty-piece symphony orchestra in the background—and I'm in a kitchen, no less—but I'm also not the kind to play around, and I know how I feel."

Her heart picked up its beat.

He went on. "To tell you the truth, I've been sure of my feelings since just about fourth grade. It's been tough watching you from far away, and now that we've come to know each other, I'm through with all that."

Steph smiled. He wasn't the man of her silly teenaged fantasies, but he was the man of her dreams. She'd tell him soon enough. Right now, she wanted to hear every word he had to say.

He didn't make her wait. "I love you. More than I can put into words. I'll always treasure you and can't imagine the rest of my life without you at my side. The way I see it, we have a great future together, so…" He reached into his chest pocket and withdrew a sparkly ring.

Steph gasped. "Oh, Hal…"

"Will you marry me?"

Tears flowed down her cheeks. Joy filled her heart. No flowery words or sweet, soaring songs could match the beauty of Hal's sincere words.

"Yes! Yes, yes, yes!"

He slipped the diamond on her ring finger, and then, with that tenderness that had charmed her from the first time he'd let her see it, Hal bent down and sealed their promise with a kiss.

How she loved this decent, godly, straightforward man! And she was going to spend the rest of her life at his side—

Bang!

"Toldja!" Granny Annie crowed. "They're smooching in the kitchen, Tabitha. Come see!"

Moments later, the kitchen was filled with well-wishers. Granny, Miss Tabitha and her gentleman friend Gordon Graver, Mason Cutler, from The Pines and the newlywed Tess led the way. Of course, everyone had to ooh and aah at her ring, slap Hal's back and give her a hug.

Soon enough, a piercing whistle cut through the loud chatter. Steph looked up. Police Chief-to-be Ethan Rodgers waved everyone out into the hall. "Results are in. Time to party, Sheriff Benson!"

Hal reached out and took Steph's hand. "Ready?"

"Oh, yeah!"

To the ringing notes of "Stars and Stripes," courtesy of the Loganton High School Marching Marauders, they stepped out onto the stage, the cheers of the crowd deafening. Holding hands, they waved and smiled.

Even though the celebration was for Hal's election, Steph would always equate balloons, a zippy march and the cheers of all their friends with the promises they'd made.

How much more romantic could a proposal get?

* * * * *

Dear Reader,

I hope you enjoyed joining Steph and Hal for this adventure. The idea for at least a portion of it has been with me ever since I started thinking of writing a book. You see, like Steph, I also have Attention Deficit Disorder, and have had to learn different ways to manage my "interesting" brain. But God has been very good to me. While ADD does present a challenge to my concentration, it also presents me with an unusual blessing: the what-ifs so necessary for writing are just the natural state of affairs inside my head—most people call it daydreaming. I call it work!

Our wonderful, loving heavenly Father never gives us more than we can handle, and often salts our difficulties with surprising flip sides. I hope you let Him bless you even through those challenging quirks that make you the unique individual you are. My prayer for you is that you hold on to the hand He holds out to all of us, so that He can see you through all your challenges.

You can contact me by e-mail at ginnyaiken@gmail.com, or on my Web site at www.ginnyaikenwrites.com.

Blessings,

Ginny Aiken

QUESTIONS FOR DISCUSSION

1. No one is perfect. Disability comes in all kinds of forms. Have you had to overcome something you can't change about yourself? How did you do it? What part did your faith play in dealing with your disability?

2. When Hal looked back on his school years, he wished he'd been able to deal with his shyness so that he could have helped Steph with her schoolwork. Is there someone you think you failed? Is there something you've done to make up for that failure? If so, what was it?

3. Steph didn't want to worry her parents so she didn't talk to them about the crime wave that hit her. In doing so, however, she limited her source of support in a tough time. How do you respond to difficult circumstances? Do you limit the blessing God has for you by your actions?

4. Hal was running for reelection, and was determined to win another term as sheriff. Not only did he have to run against his declared opponent, he also had to deal with a potential write-in challenge. How would you respond to that kind of double-pronged test? How would you deal with a venomous opponent like Ed?

5. Small towns often have a "hub" where residents congregate on a regular basis. In Loganton, the church and Granny Annie's Diner are the twin hubs. Is there a similar hub where you live? If so, what benefit do you and others

gain from it? Is there anything you can do to make it more of a blessing?

6. Steph and Darcy were friends since grade school. Steph trusts Darcy implicitly. Do you have a friend like that? How have you nurtured that friendship over the years? What does it mean to you now in adulthood?

7. Darcy's mother's illness makes her desperate enough to turn to the "easy" answer: crime. Her lack of faith made her vulnerable to that kind of lifestyle. Is there anything that would challenge your sense of right and wrong to that extent? How would you have responded in Darcy's situation?

8. As close as Darcy and Steph are, Darcy harbors a sense of envy toward Steph. Is there someone in your life who you see as having an easier time than you? Is there a chance you've missed how hard life seems to her? How will you go forward now?

9. Have you ever been betrayed by someone you trust as completely as Steph trusted Darcy? If so, how have you handled the betrayal? Is there anything you now know you should have done but didn't? If so, can you still do it?

10. I'm very much a pet person—I have a Sun Conure parrot and two dogs—and can't imagine living alone as Steph did. Have you shared your life with a nonhuman critter? If so, how does God work through these members of His creation in your life? If not, how do you respond to His nonhuman creatures?

11. Drug abuse has become a horrible reality in our society. Has it touched your life, and if so, how? What was your response?

12. Forgiveness is one of the toughest doctrines of our faith, and it must have been even more of a challenge for Steph to forgive Darcy because of their long friendship. Have you been called to forgive someone you love for something serious? How did you handle your emotions? How did your faith impact your actions?

REQUEST YOUR FREE BOOKS!

2 FREE RIVETING INSPIRATIONAL NOVELS
PLUS 2 FREE MYSTERY GIFTS

YES! Please send me 2 FREE Love Inspired® Suspense novels and my 2 FREE mystery gifts (gifts are worth about $10). After receiving them, if I don't wish to receive any more books, I can return the shipping statement marked "cancel". If I don't cancel, I will receive 4 brand-new novels every month and be billed just $4.24 per book in the U.S. or $4.74 per book in Canada, plus 25¢ shipping and handling per book and applicable taxes, if any*. That's a savings of over 20% off the cover price! I understand that accepting the 2 free books and gifts places me under no obligation to buy anything. I can always return a shipment and cancel at any time. Even if I never buy another book, the two free books and gifts are mine to keep forever.

123 IDN ERXX   323 IDN ERXM

Name	(PLEASE PRINT)

Address	Apt. #

City	State/Prov.	Zip/Postal Code

Signature (if under 18, a parent or guardian must sign)

Order online at www.LoveInspiredSuspense.com
Or mail to Steeple Hill Reader Service:
IN U.S.A.: P.O. Box 1867, Buffalo, NY 14240-1867
IN CANADA: P.O. Box 609, Fort Erie, Ontario L2A 5X3

Not valid to current subscribers of Love Inspired Suspense books.

Want to try two free books from another series?
Call 1-800-873-8635 or visit www.morefreebooks.com

* Terms and prices subject to change without notice. N.Y. residents add applicable sales tax. Canadian residents will be charged applicable provincial taxes and GST. Offer not valid in Quebec. This offer is limited to one order per household. All orders subject to approval. Credit or debit balances in a customer's account(s) may be offset by any other outstanding balance owed by or to the customer. Please allow 4 to 6 weeks for delivery. Offer available while quantities last.

Your Privacy: Steeple Hill Books is committed to protecting your privacy. Our Privacy Policy is available online at www.SteepleHill.com or upon request from the Reader Service. From time to time we make our lists of customers available to reputable third parties who may have a product or service of interest to you. If you would prefer we not share your name and address, please check here.

LISUS08R

Love Inspired®
SUSPENSE

TITLES AVAILABLE NEXT MONTH

Don't miss these four stories in January

HEART OF THE NIGHT by Lenora Worth
When secret agent Eli Trudeau discovers his son is alive,
he's furious with Gena Malone, the boy's adoptive mother.
Yet even his anger can't blind him to Gena's love for the
boy. And when someone dangerous comes after them,
Eli will do *anything* to protect his newfound family.

WHAT SARAH SAW by Margaret Daley
Without a Trace

The three-year-old witness is FBI agent Sam Pierce's
best resource when the girl's mother vanishes. Yet child
psychologist Jocelyn Gold will barely let him near Sarah.
Or herself. But for the child's sake—and her mother's—
Sam and Jocelyn must join forces to uncover just what
Sarah saw.

BAYOU BETRAYAL by Robin Caroll
Monique Harris has found her father—in prison
for murder. Still, when Monique is suddenly widowed,
she seeks refuge in the bayou town of Lagniappe, not
knowing *someone* doesn't want her to stay. Deputy sheriff
Gary Anderson has Monique hoping for a new future...
if she can lay the past to rest.

FLASHOVER by Dana Mentink
Firefighter Ivy Beria is frustrated when she's injured on the
job...until she realizes the fire was no accident. The danger
builds when her neighbor disappears. With the help of
friend and colleague Tim Carnelli, Ivy starts searching for
answers, but she might find something more—like love.

LISCNM1208BPA